GRONK™

a monster's story

volume 2

a comic by katie cook

colors for the interior pages by kevin minor

the cast of gronk

kitteh:
stuffed

kitty:
cat

gronk:
monster. cute

dale:
nerd. awesome

harli:
newfie. slobbery

did you know?

-gronk is a webcomic? you can read it every friday at
www.gronkcomic.com. really, you can read a new comic every week!

-you can visit katie and her artwork online at www.katiecandraw.com?

-that gronk volume 1 is a delightful book and, if you do not own it, is
a purchase you will not regret?

-you can visit kevin online at www.universe-m.com

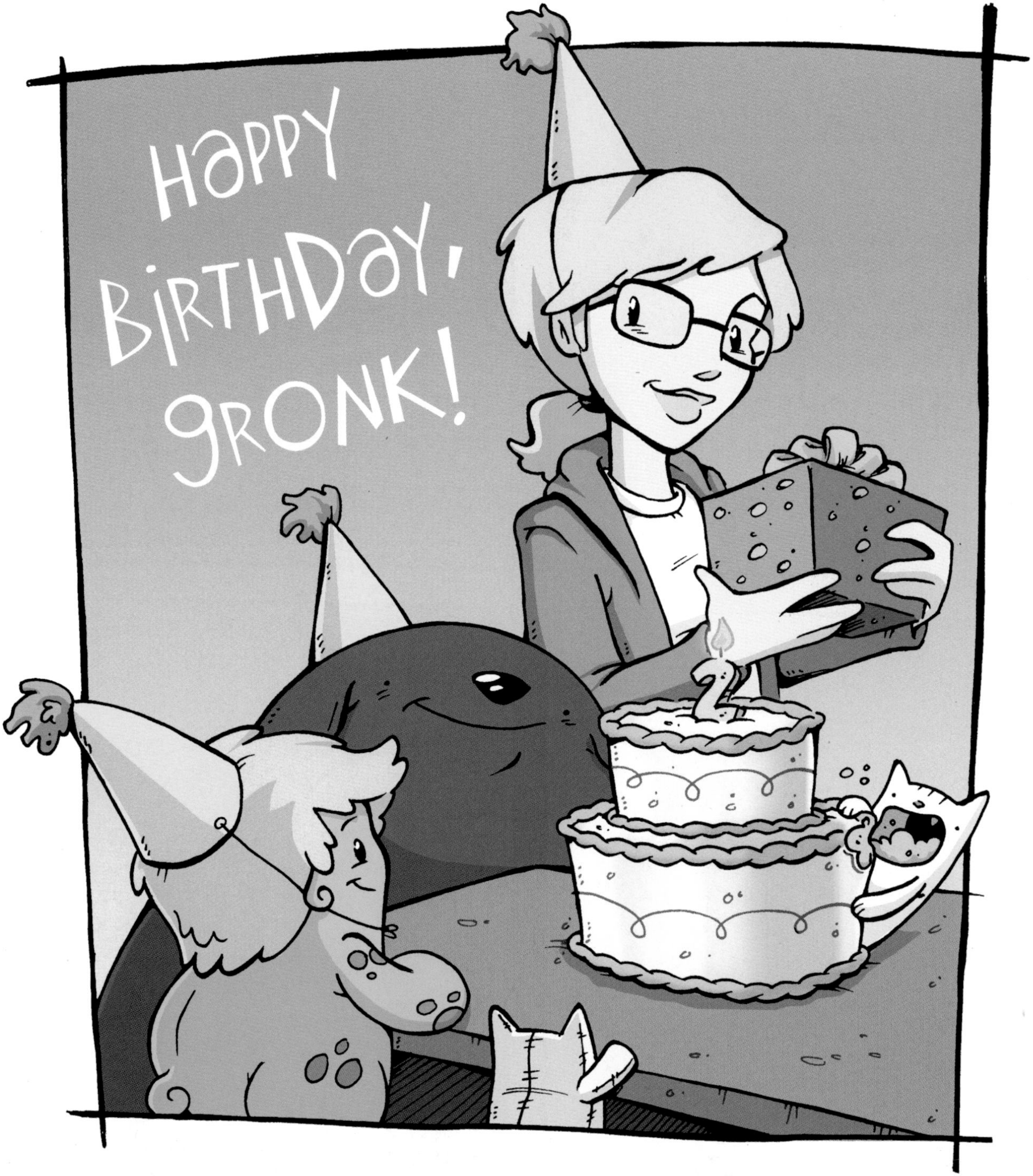
HAPPY BIRTHDAY, GRONK!

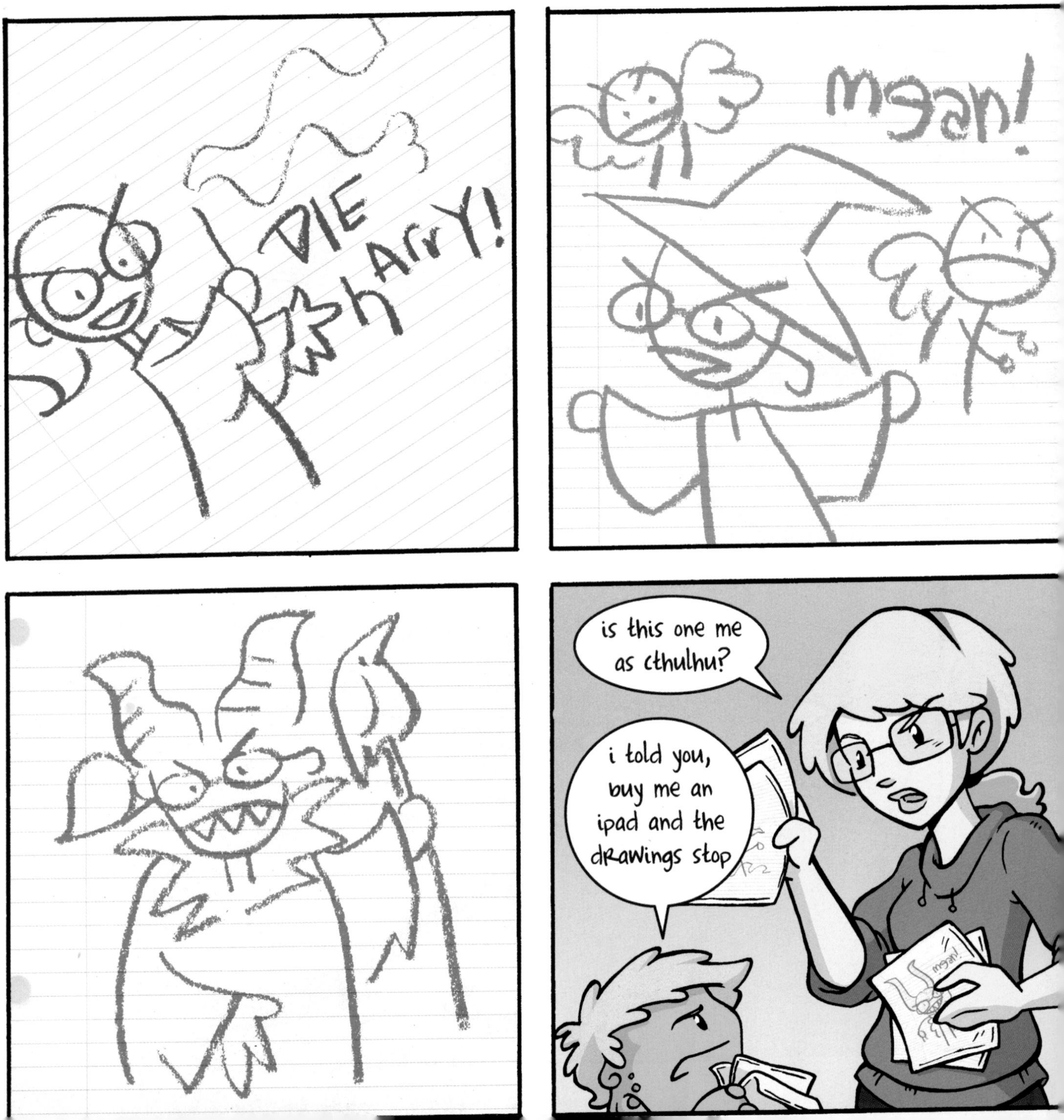
DIE hArrY!
mean!
is this one me as cthulhu?
i told you, buy me an ipad and the drawings stop

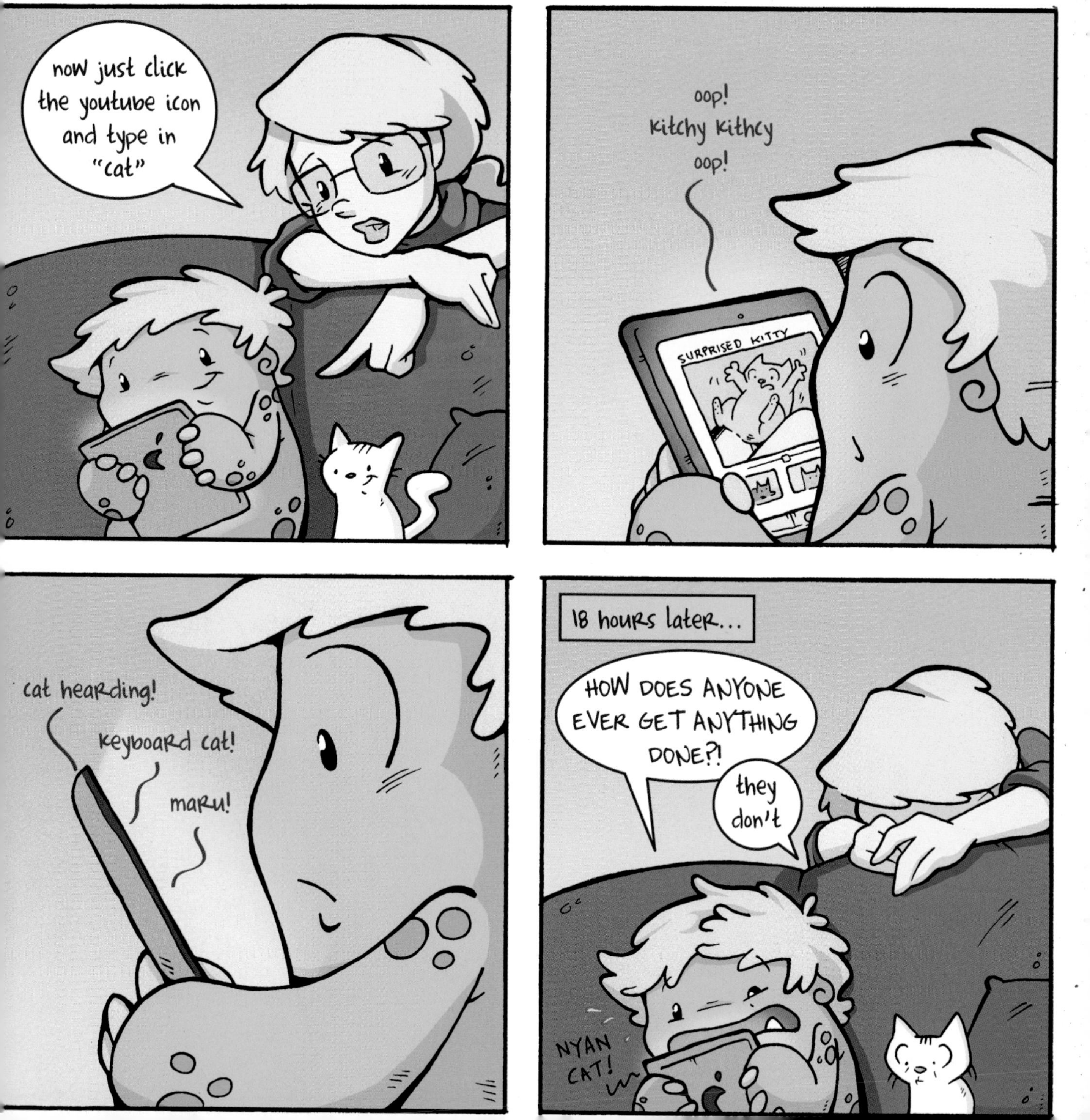
now just click the youtube icon and type in "cat"
oop! kitchy kithcy oop!
SURPRISED KITTY
cat hearding!
keyboard cat!
maru!
18 hours later...
HOW DOES ANYONE EVER GET ANYTHING DONE?!
they don't
NYAN CAT!

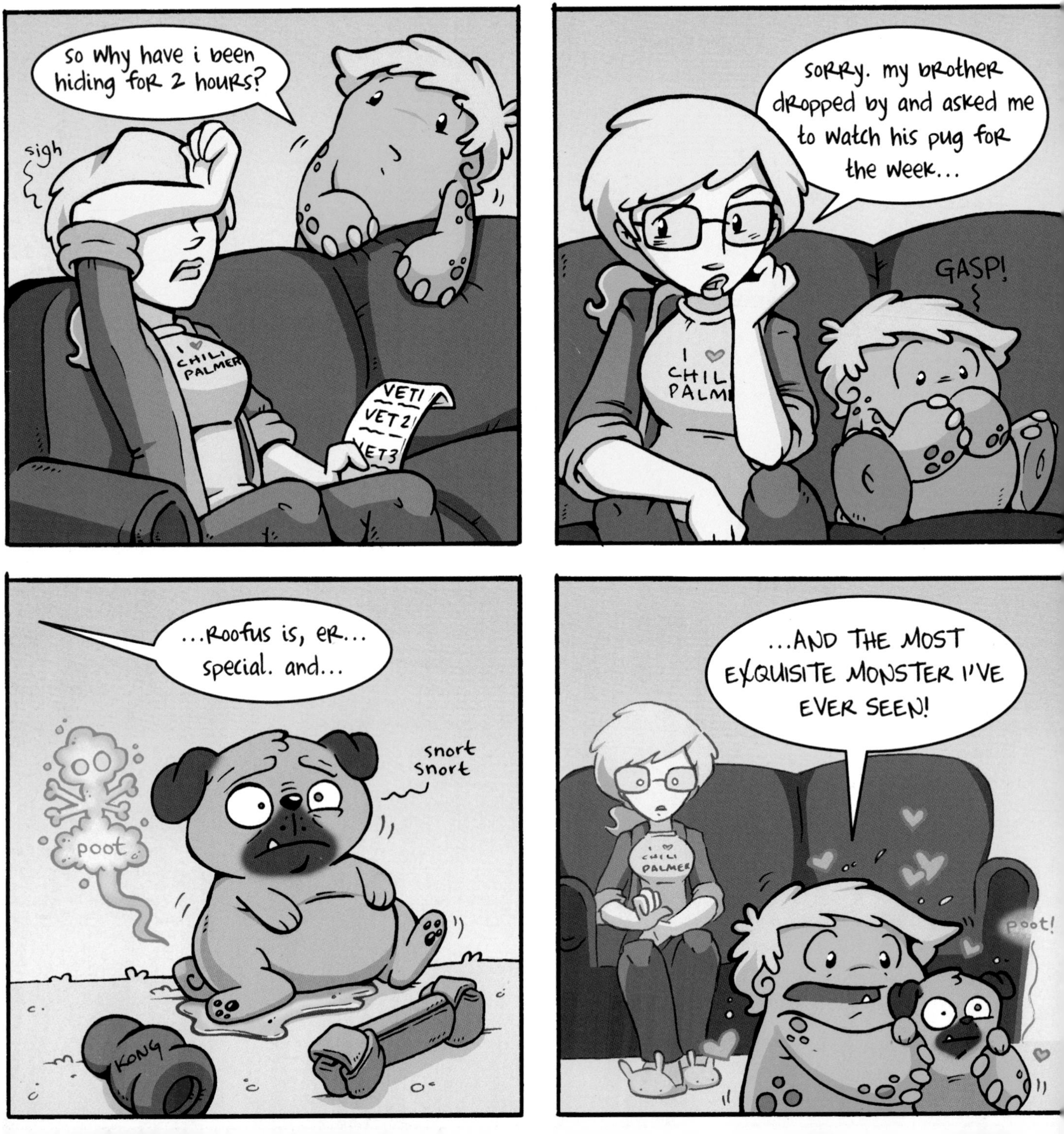
so why have i been hiding for 2 hours?
sigh
I ♥ CHILI PALMER
VET1
VET2
VET3
sorry. my brother dropped by and asked me to watch his pug for the week...
GASP!
I ♥ CHILI PALM
...Roofus is, er... special. and...
poot
snort snort
KONG
...AND THE MOST EXQUISITE MONSTER I'VE EVER SEEN!
I ♥ CHILI PALMER
poot!

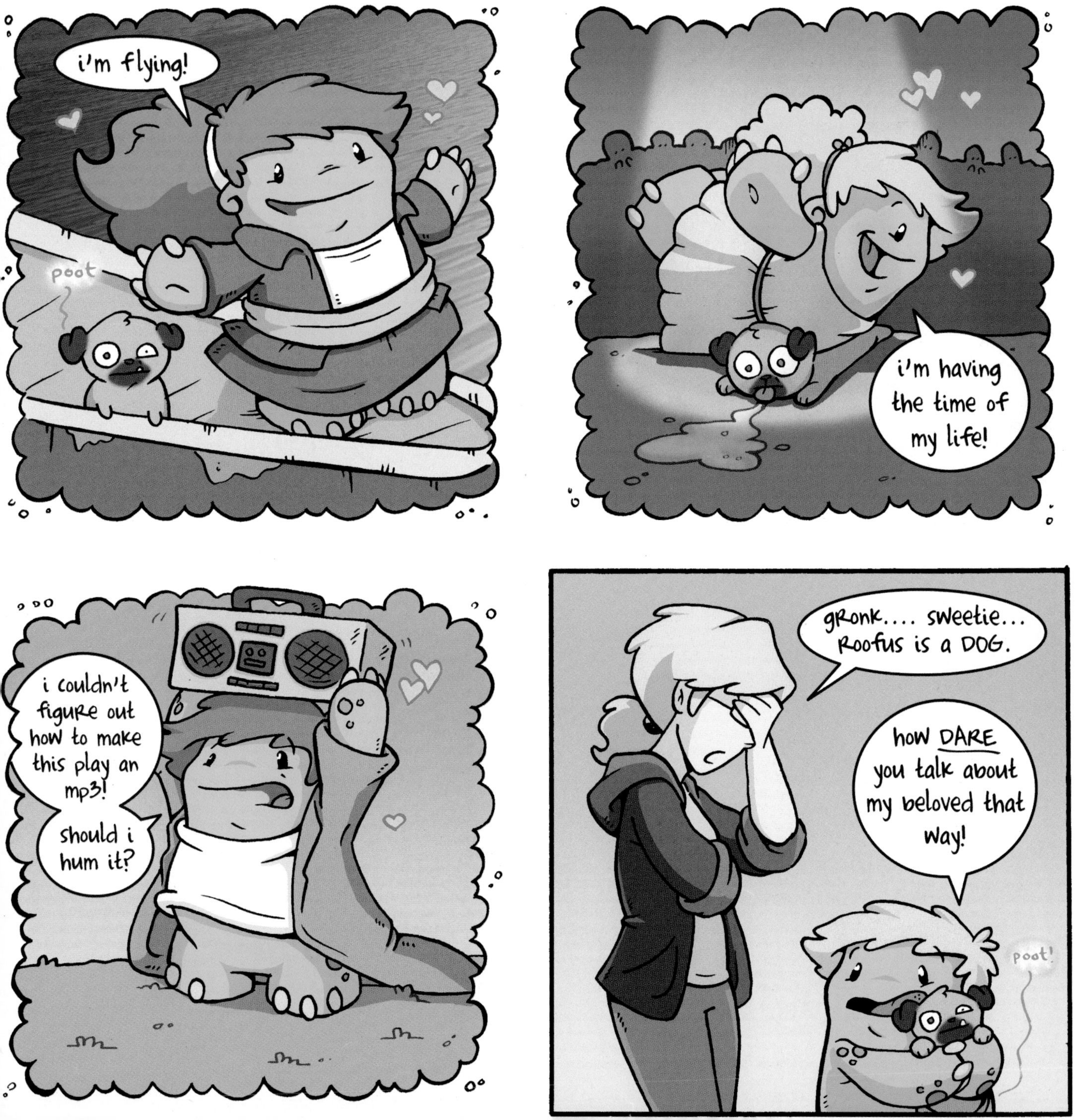
i'm flying!
poot
i'm having the time of my life!
i couldn't figure out how to make this play an mp3!
should i hum it?
gronk.... sweetie... roofus is a DOG.
how DARE you talk about my beloved that way!
poot!

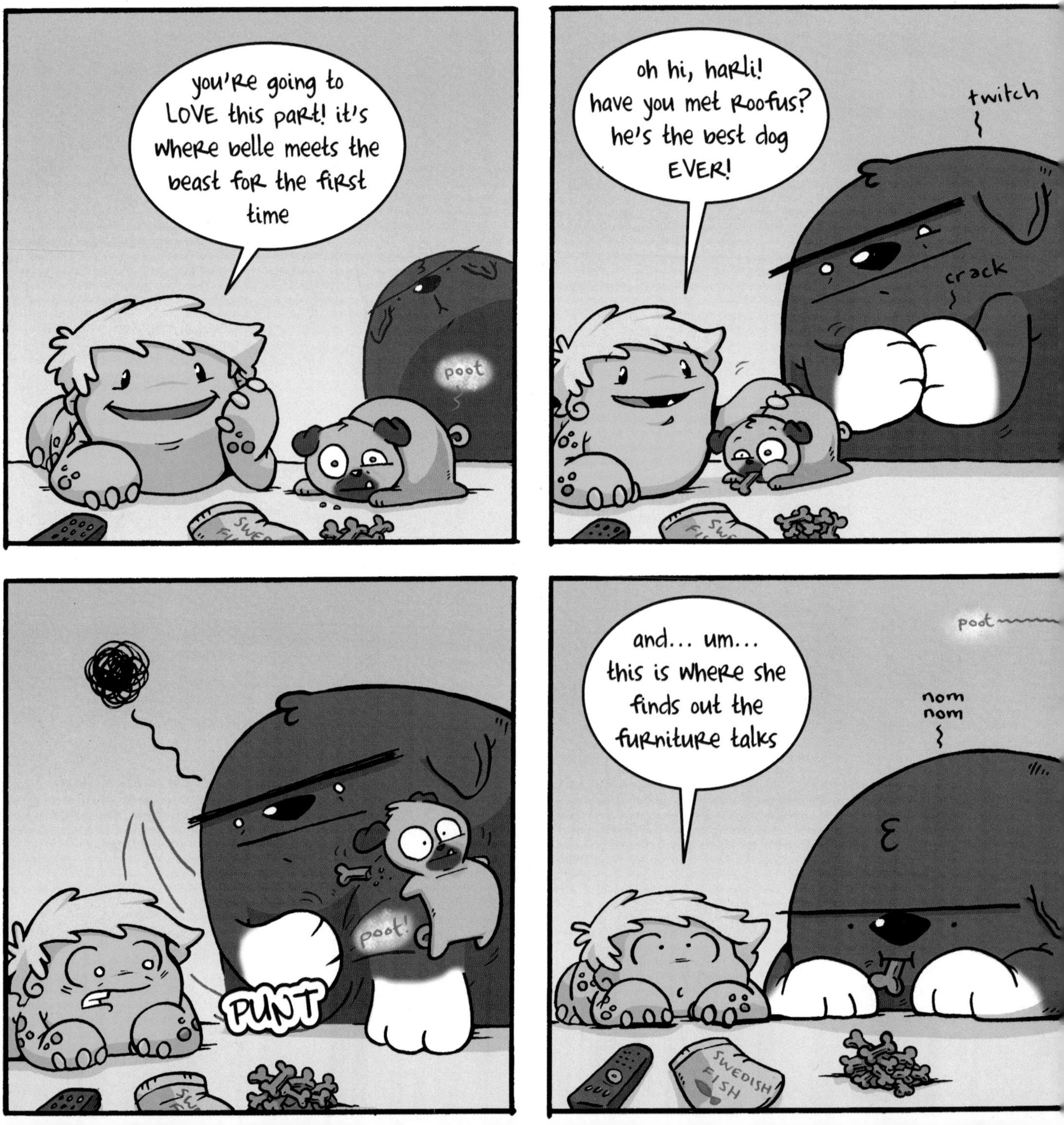
you're going to LOVE this part! it's where belle meets the beast for the first time
poot
oh hi, harli! have you met Roofus? he's the best dog EVER!
twitch
crack
poot!
PUNT
and... um... this is where she finds out the furniture talks
poot
nom nom
SWEDISH FISH

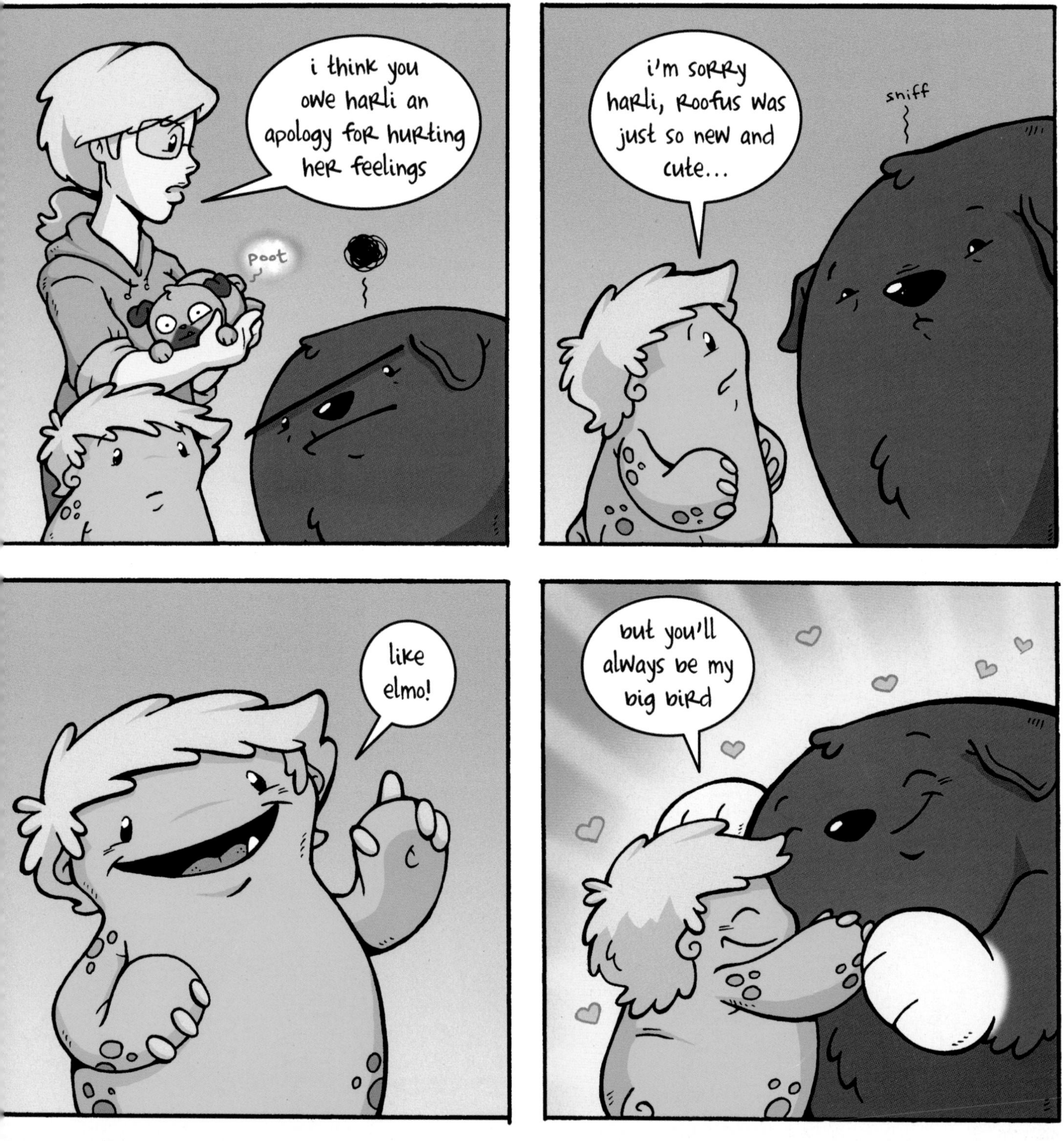
i think you owe harli an apology for hurting her feelings
poot
i'm sorry harli, Roofus was just so new and cute...
sniff
like elmo!
but you'll always be my big bird

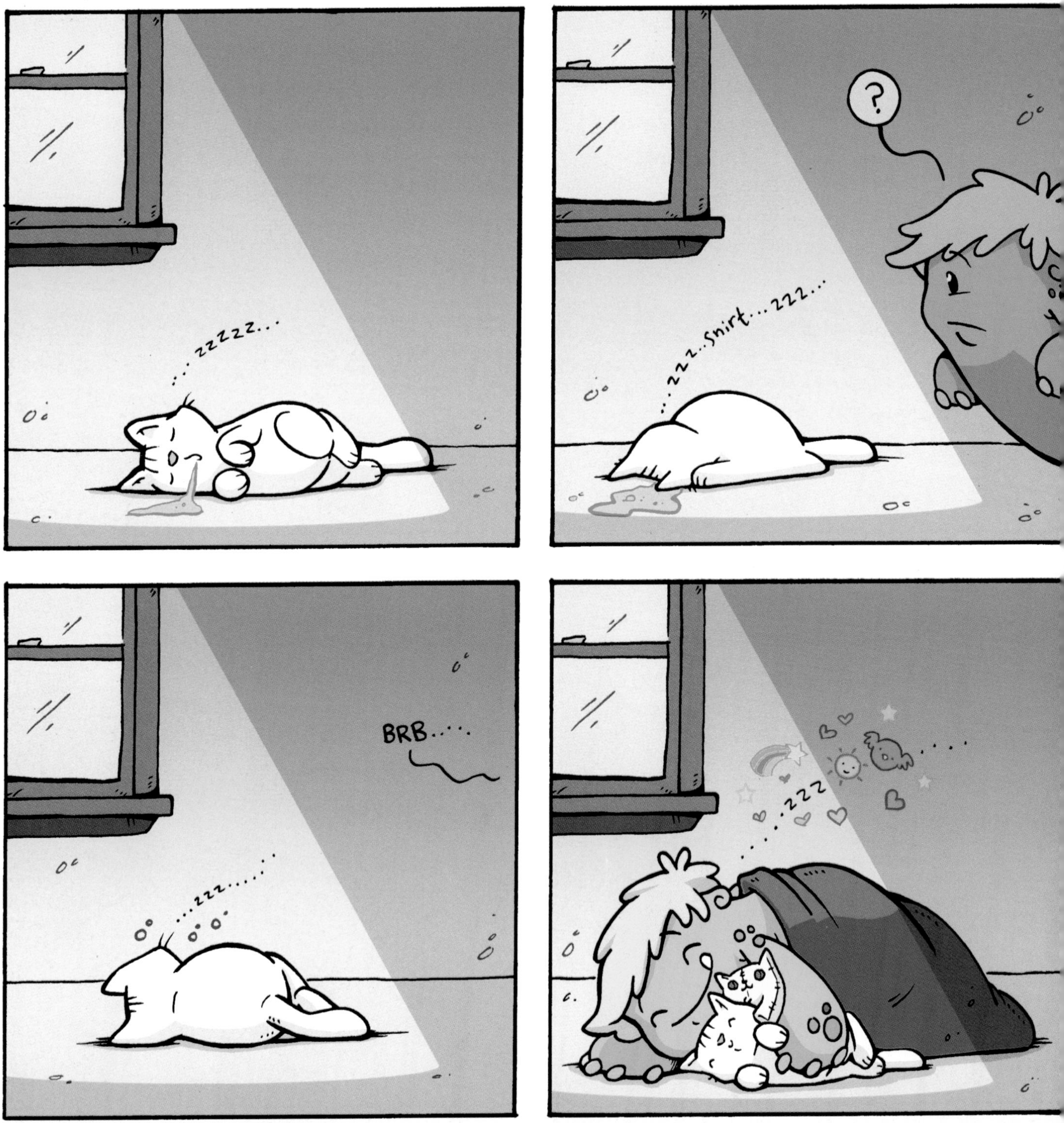
...zzzzz...
...zzz..snirt...zzz...
?
...zzz.....
BRB.....
...zzz

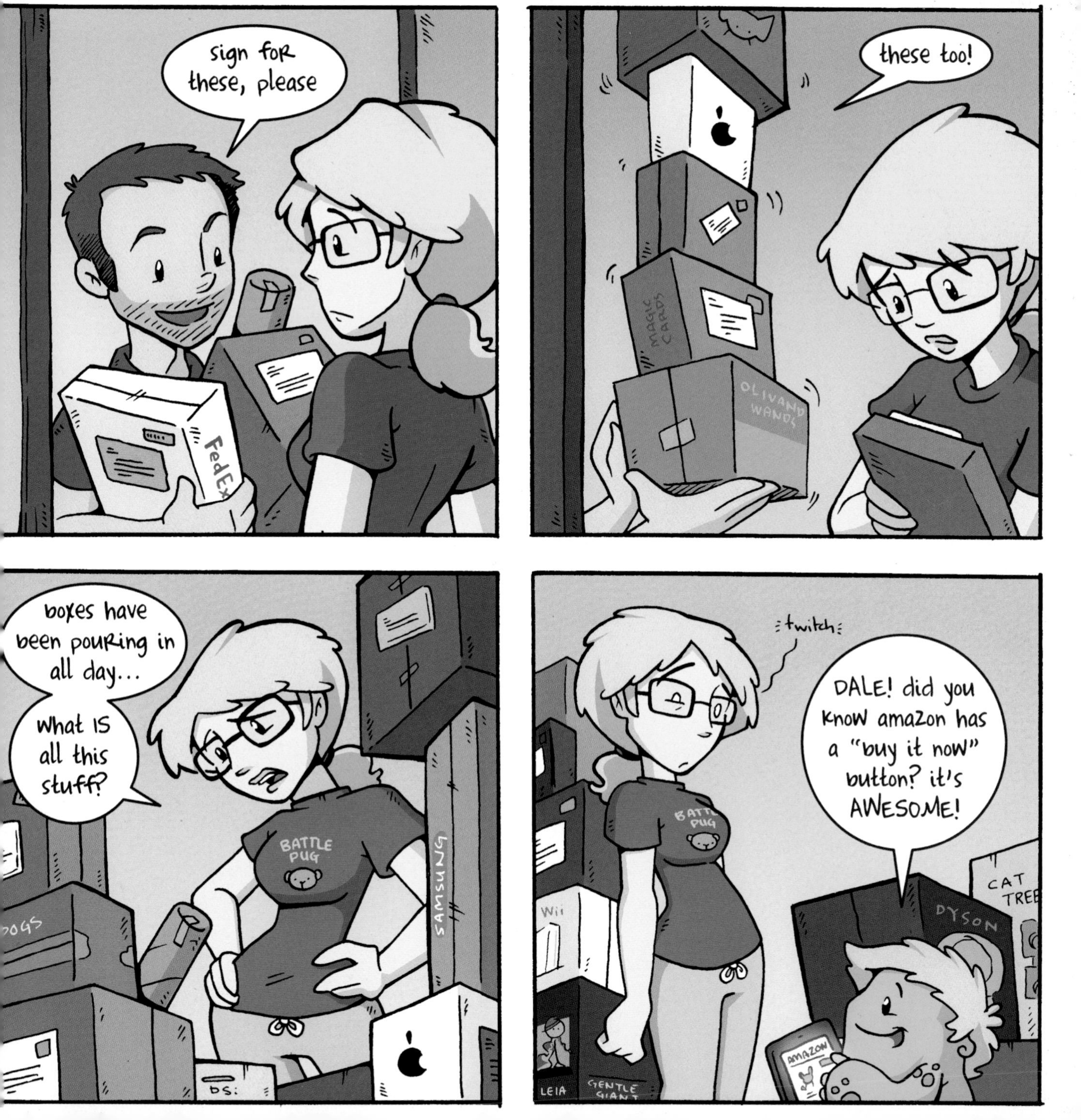
sign for these, please
FedEx
these too!
MAGIC CARDS
OLIVAND WANDS
boxes have been pouring in all day...
What IS all this stuff?
BATTLE PUG
SAMSUNG
DS:
:twitch:
DALE! did you know amazon has a "buy it now" button? it's AWESOME!
BATTLE PUG
Wii
CAT TREE
DYSON
AMAZON
LEIA
GENTLE GIANT

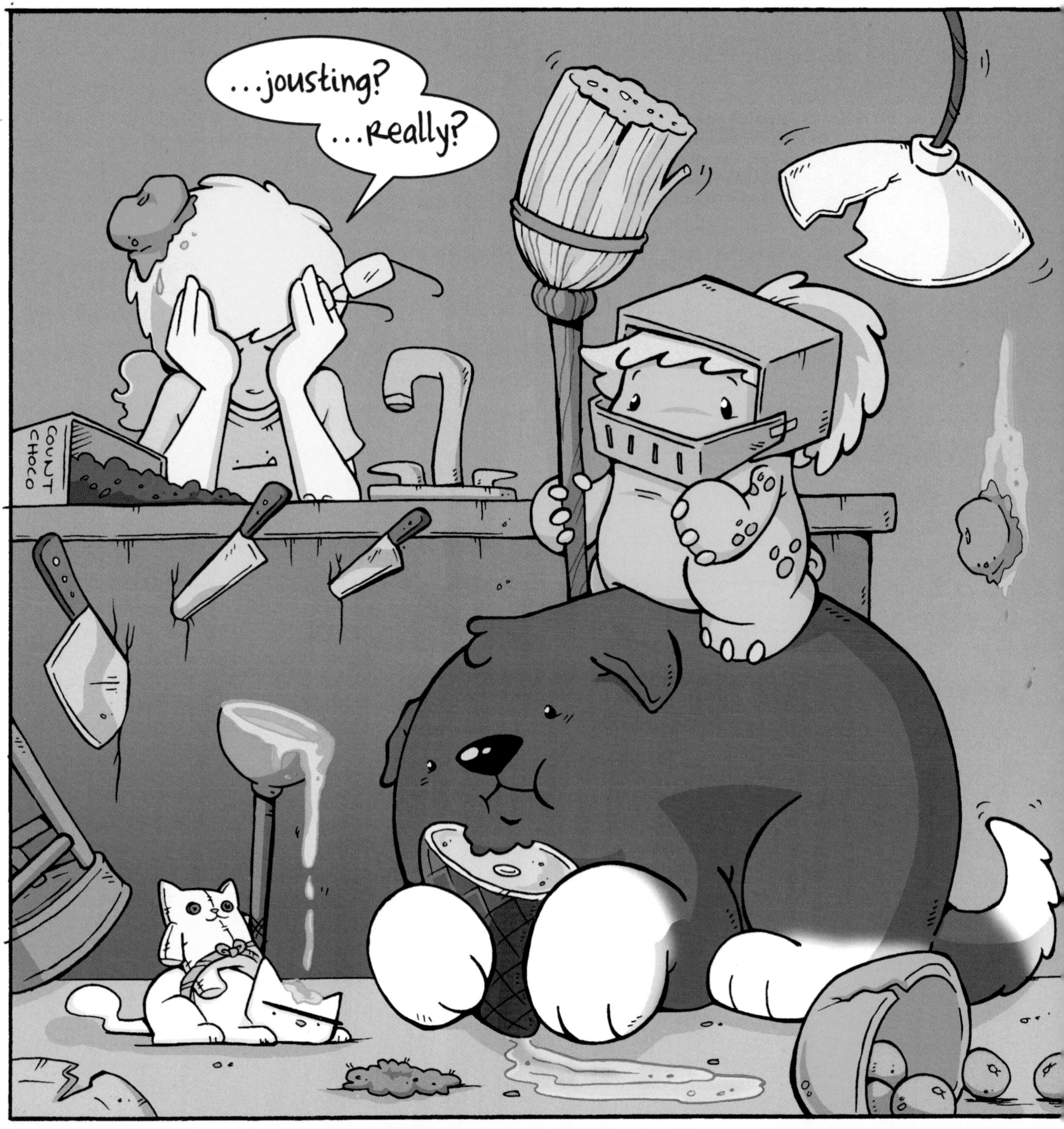
...jousting?
...Really?
COUNT CHOCO

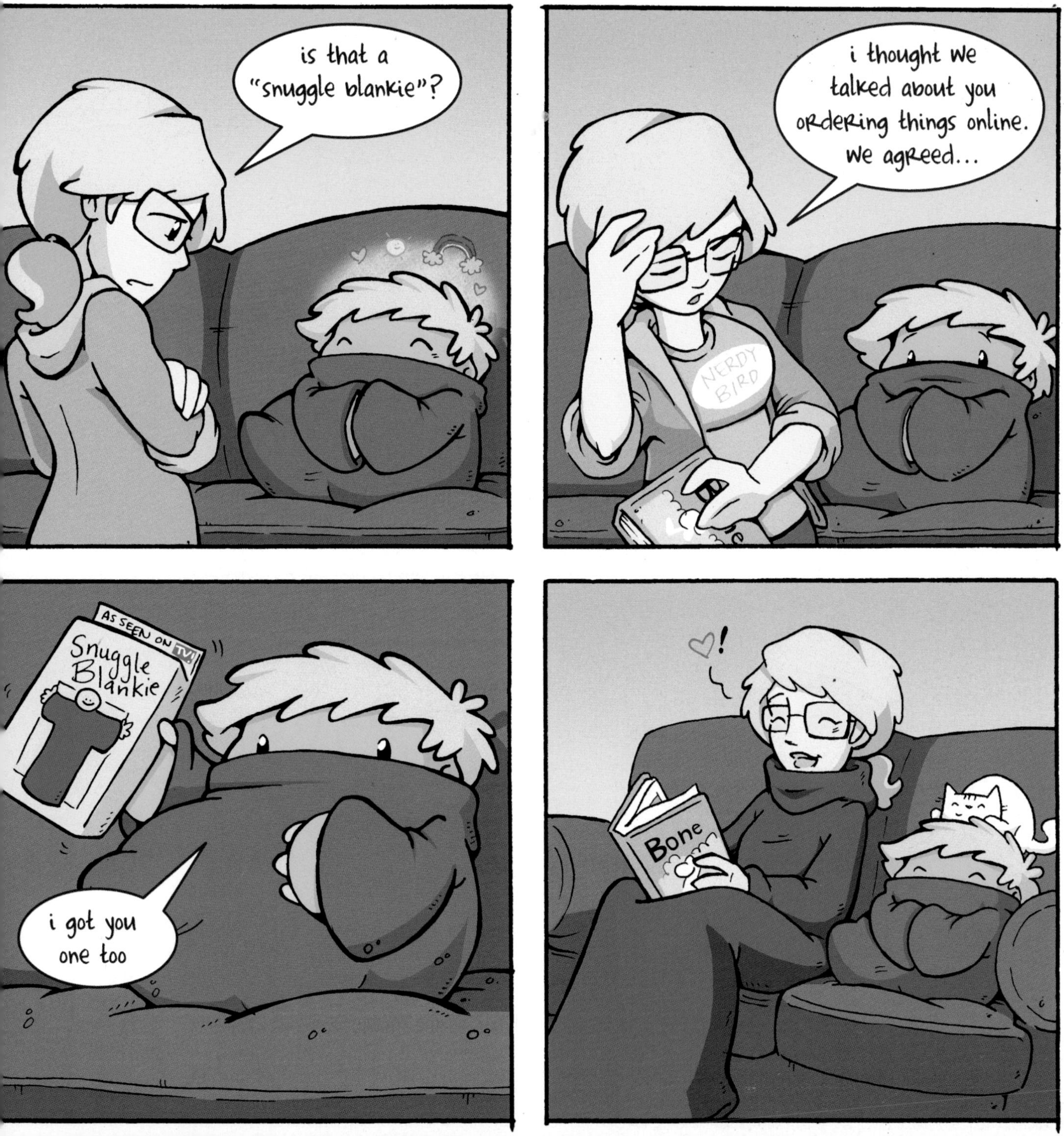
is that a "snuggle blankie"?
i thought we talked about you ordering things online. we agreed...
AS SEEN ON TV!
Snuggle Blankie
i got you one too
Bone

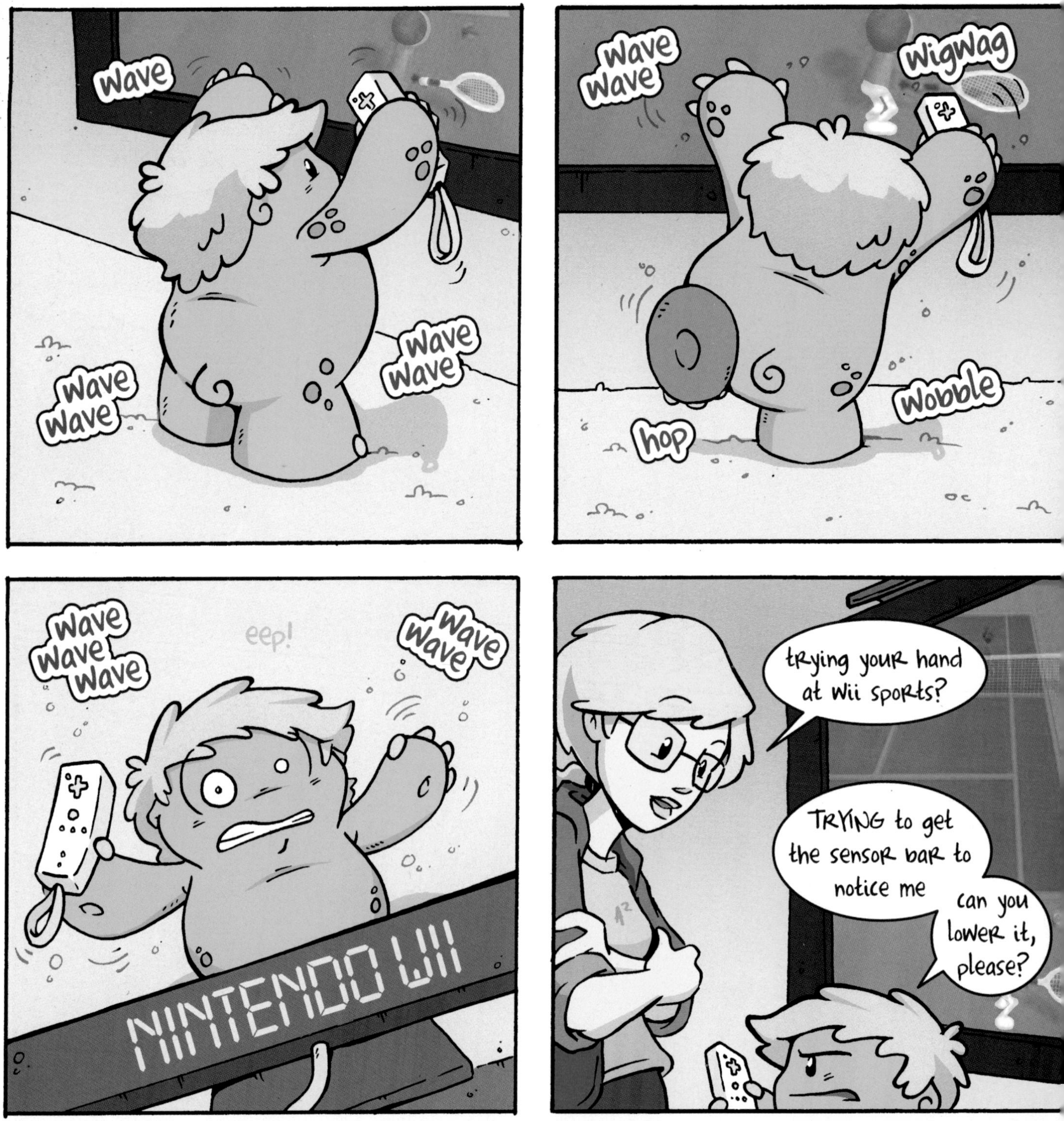
Wave
Wave Wave
Wave Wave
Wave Wave
Wigwag
hop
Wobble
Wave Wave Wave
eep!
Wave Wave
NINTENDO Wii
trying your hand at Wii sports?
TRYING to get the sensor bar to notice me
can you lower it, please?

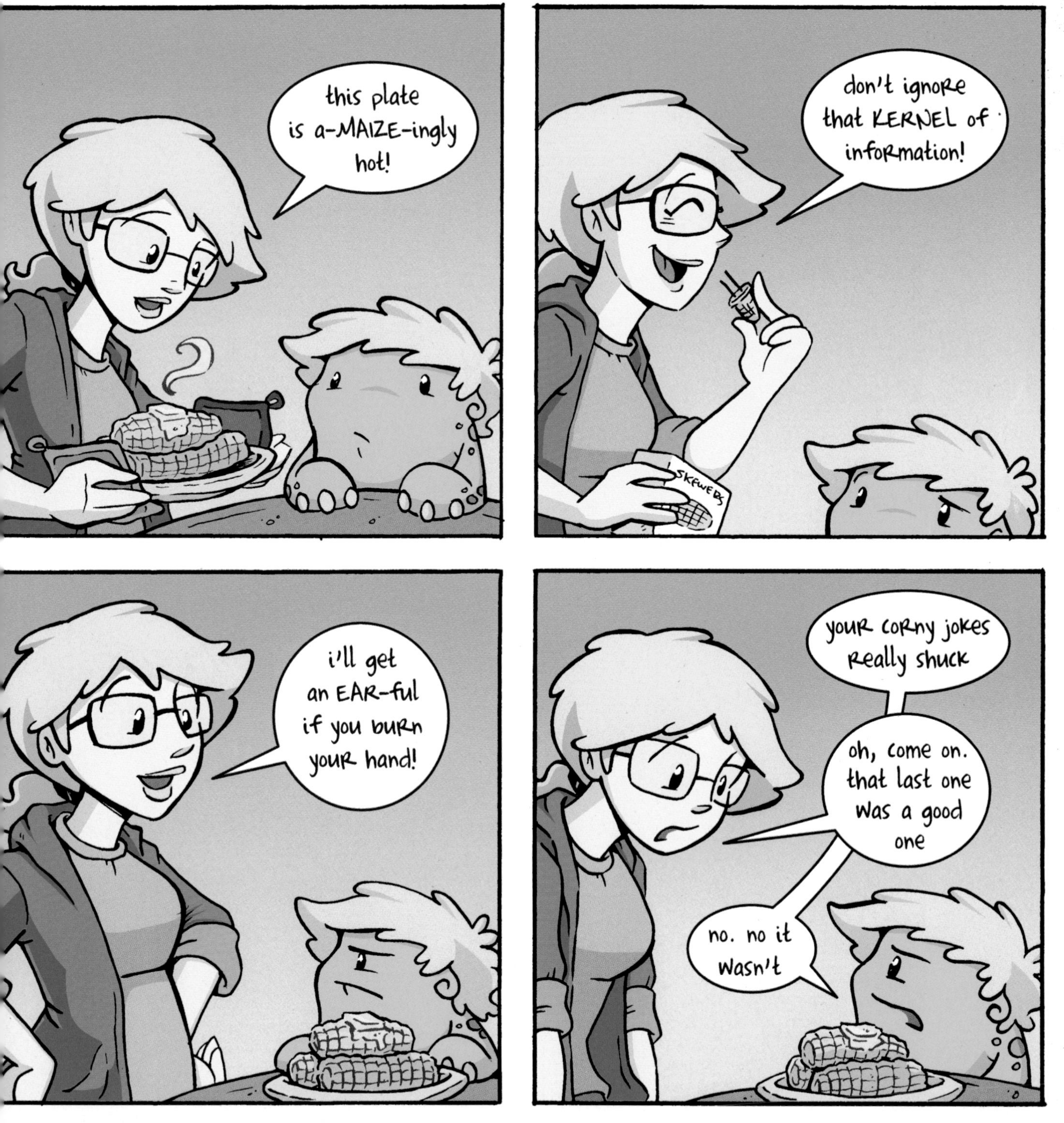
this plate is a-MAIZE-ingly hot!
don't ignore that KERNEL of information!
SKEWERS
i'll get an EAR-ful if you burn your hand!
your corny jokes really shuck
oh, come on. that last one was a good one
no. no it wasn't

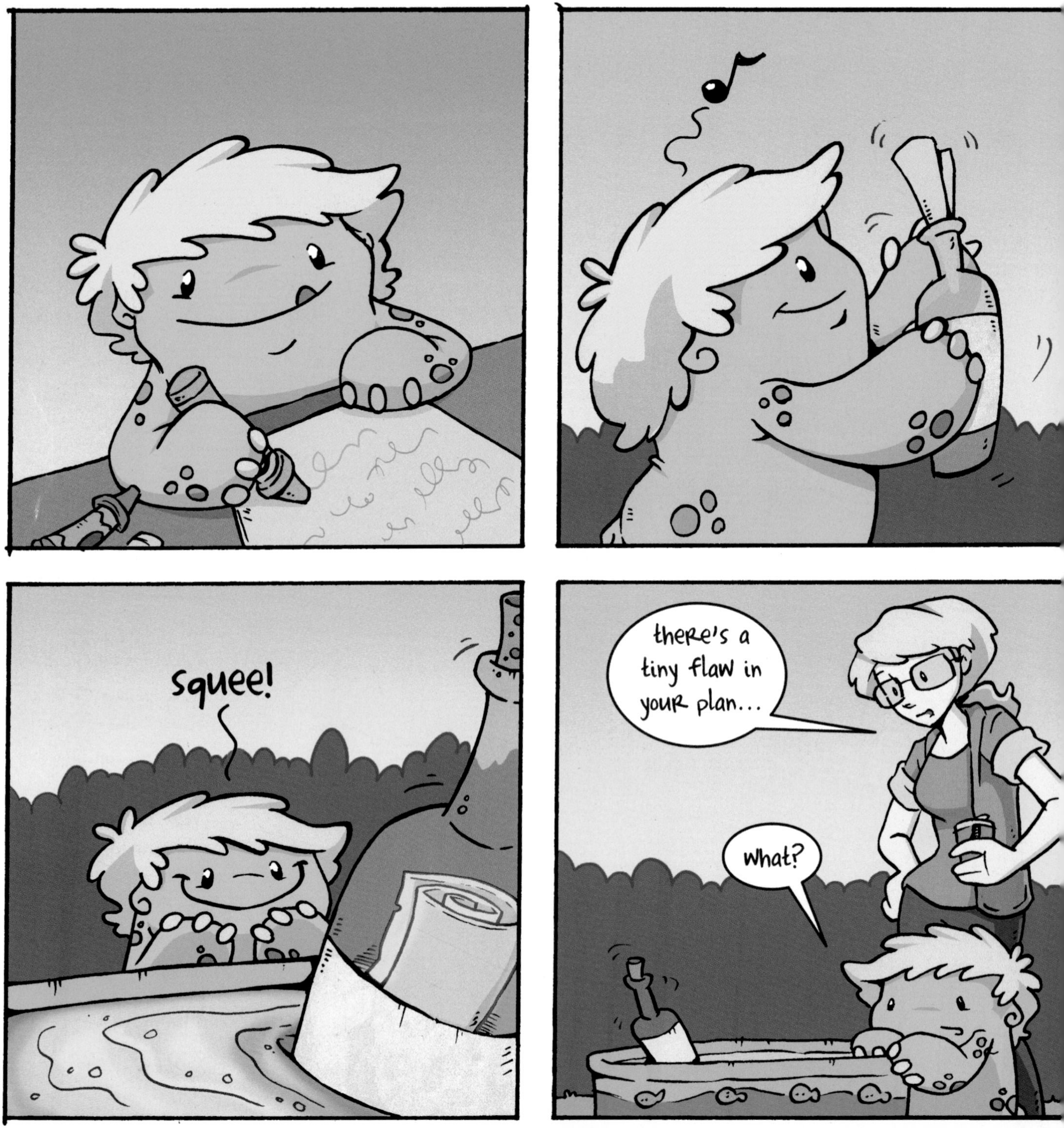
squee!
there's a tiny flaw in your plan...
what?

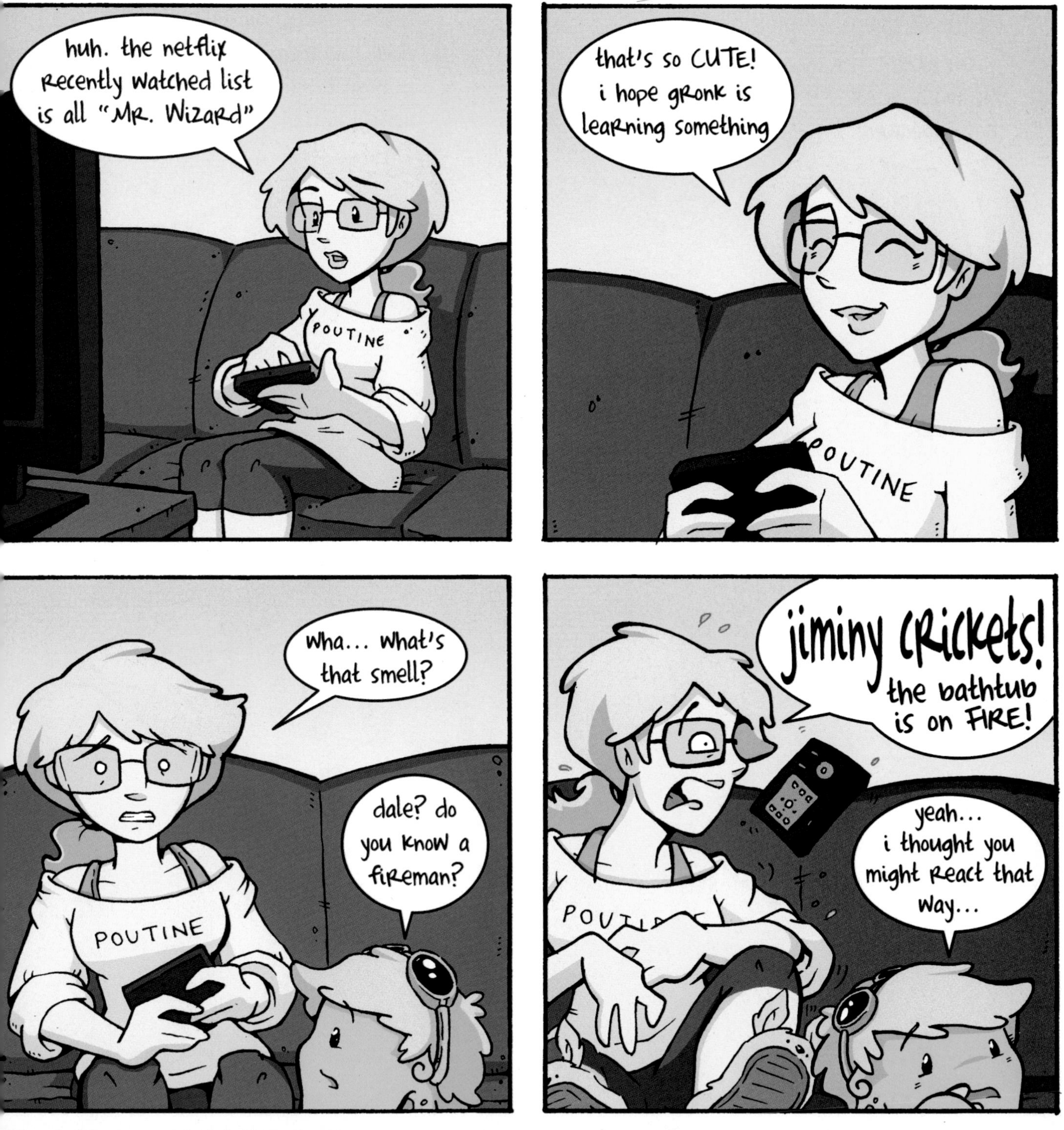
huh. the netflix recently watched list is all "Mr. Wizard"
that's so CUTE! i hope gronk is learning something
wha... what's that smell?
dale? do you know a fireman?
jiminy crickets! the bathtub is on FIRE!
yeah... i thought you might react that way...

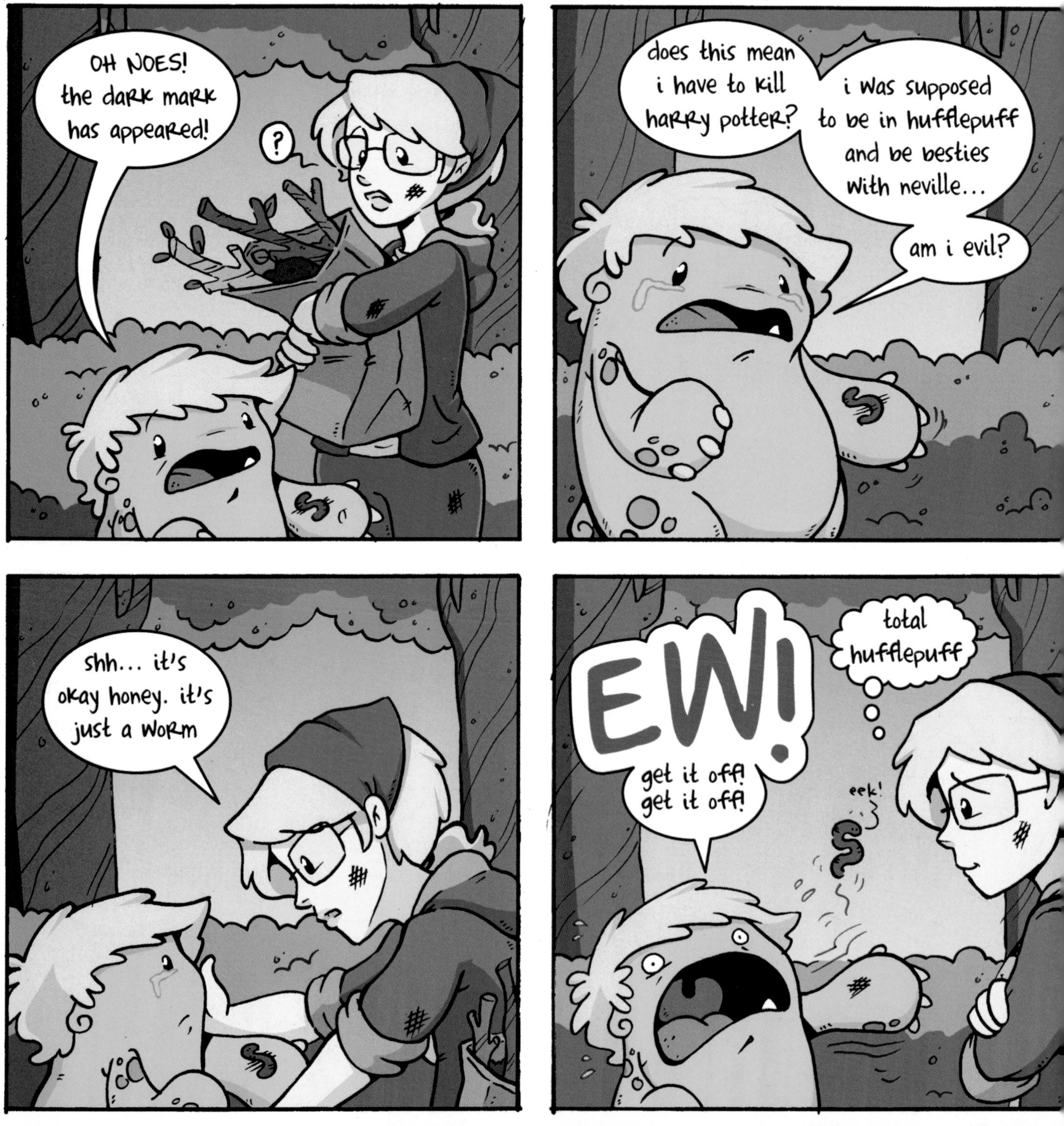
OH NOES!
the dark mark
has appeared!
?
does this mean
i have to kill
harry potter?
i was supposed
to be in hufflepuff
and be besties
with neville...
am i evil?
shh... it's
okay honey. it's
just a worm
EW!
get it off!
get it off!
total
hufflepuff
eek!

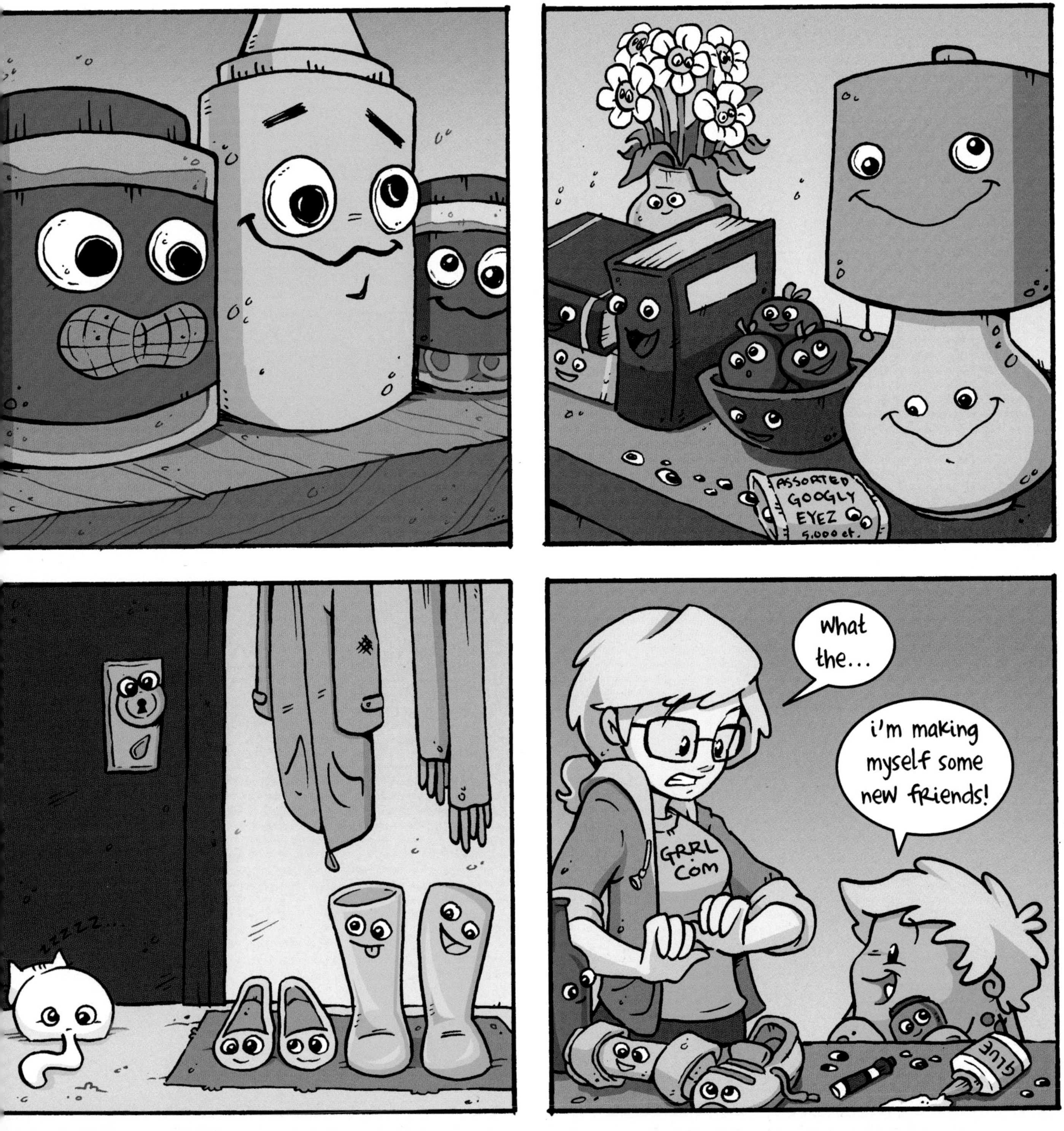
ASSORTED
GOOGLY
EYEZ
5,000 ct.
zzzzz...
What the...
i'm making myself some new friends!
GRRL COM
GLUE

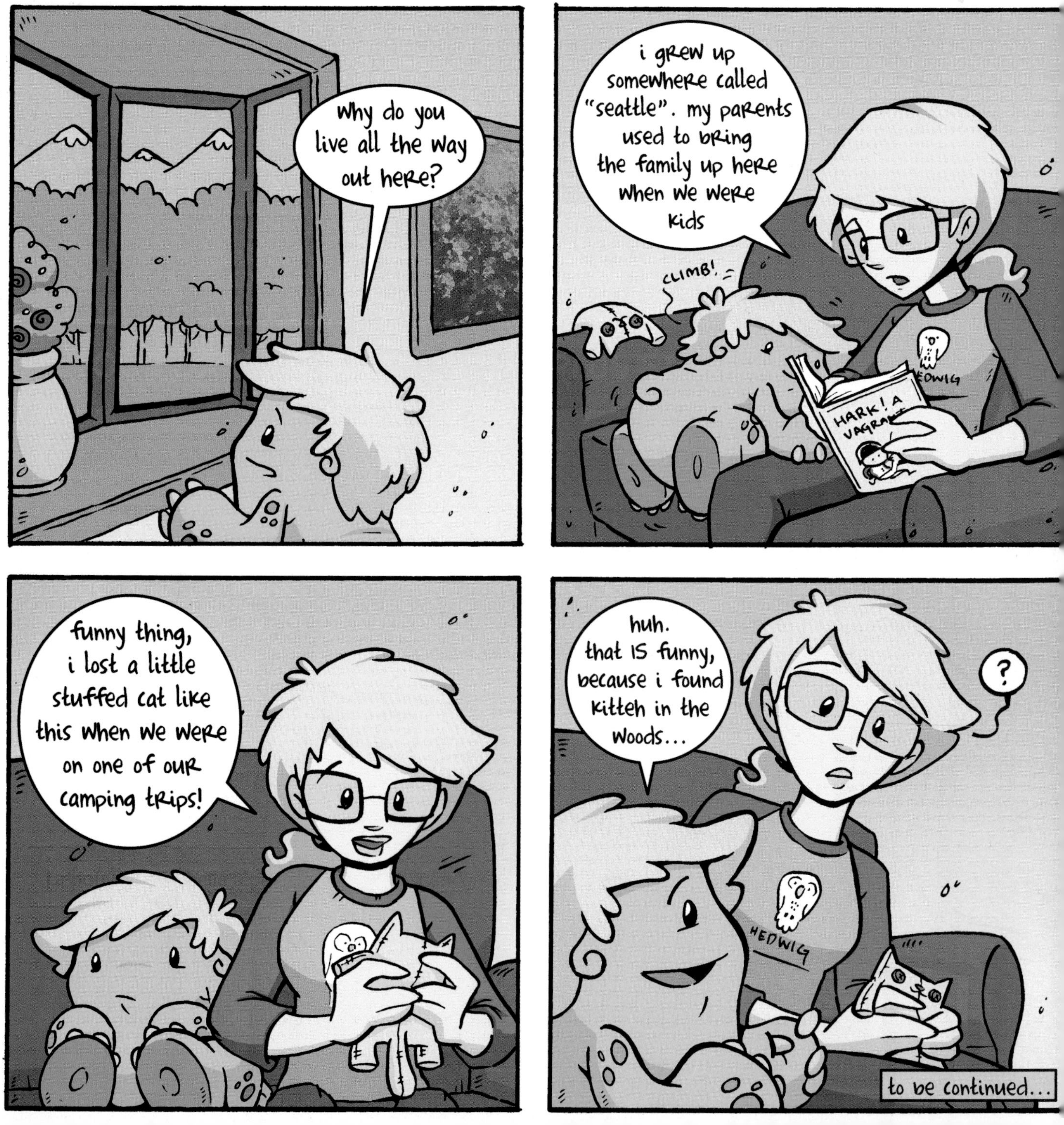
why do you live all the way out here?
i grew up somewhere called "seattle". my parents used to bring the family up here when we were kids
CLIMB!
HEDWIG
HARK! A VAGRA
funny thing, i lost a little stuffed cat like this when we were on one of our camping trips!
huh. that IS funny, because i found kitteh in the woods...
?
HEDWIG
to be continued...

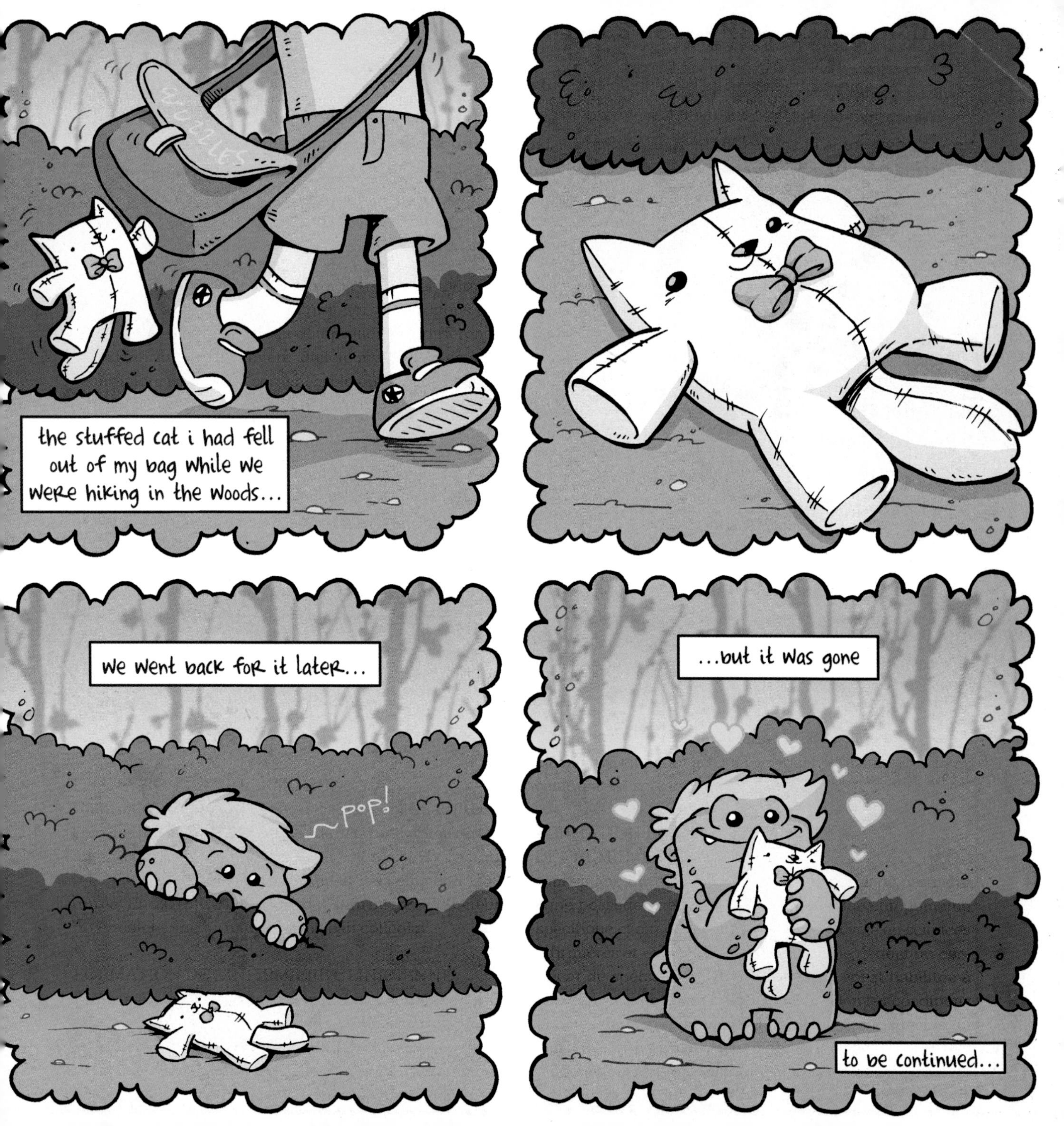
the stuffed cat i had fell out of my bag while we were hiking in the woods...
we went back for it later...
~POP!
...but it was gone
to be continued...

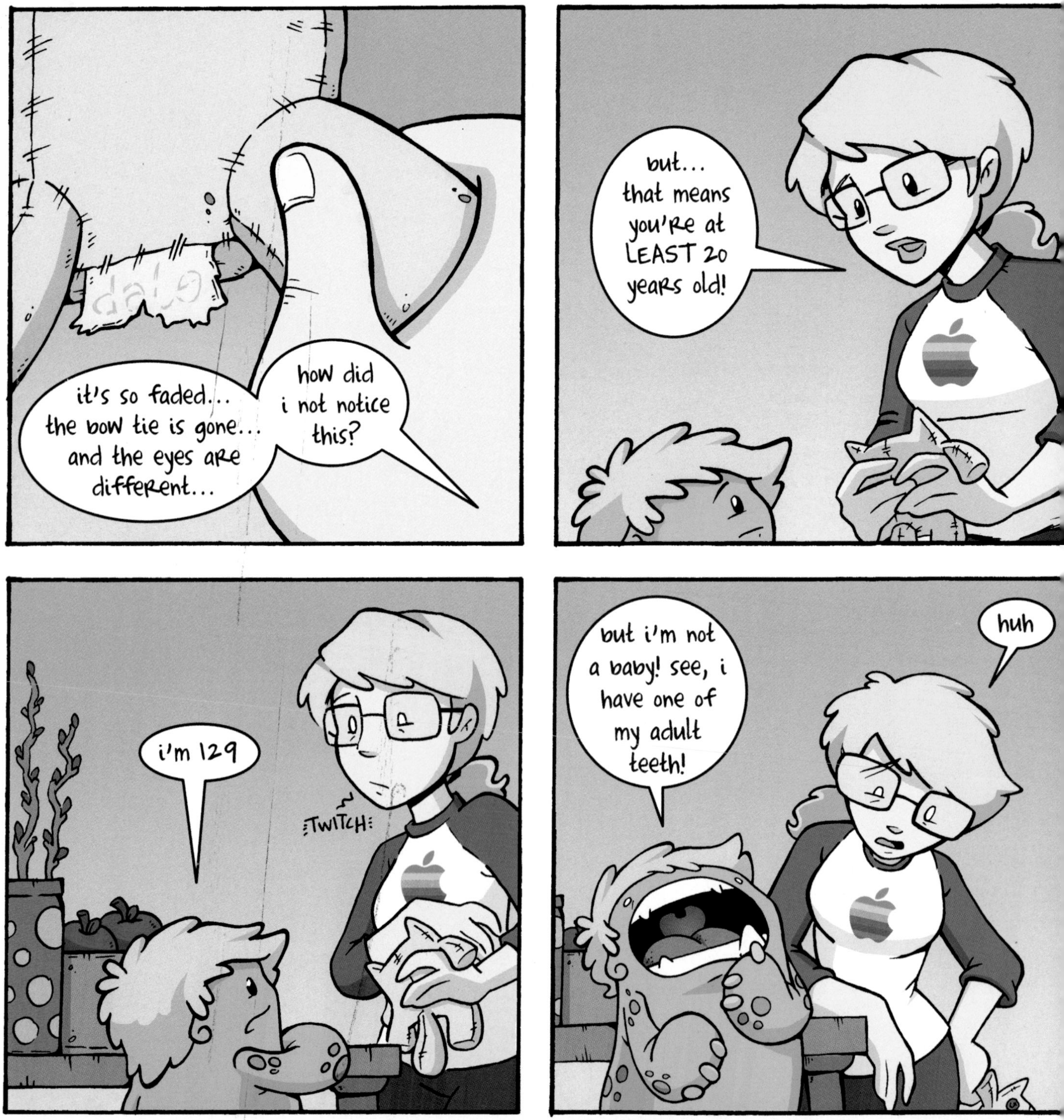
dale
it's so faded...
the bow tie is gone...
and the eyes are different...
how did i not notice this?
but... that means you're at LEAST 20 years old!
i'm 129
TWITCH
but i'm not a baby! see, i have one of my adult teeth!
huh

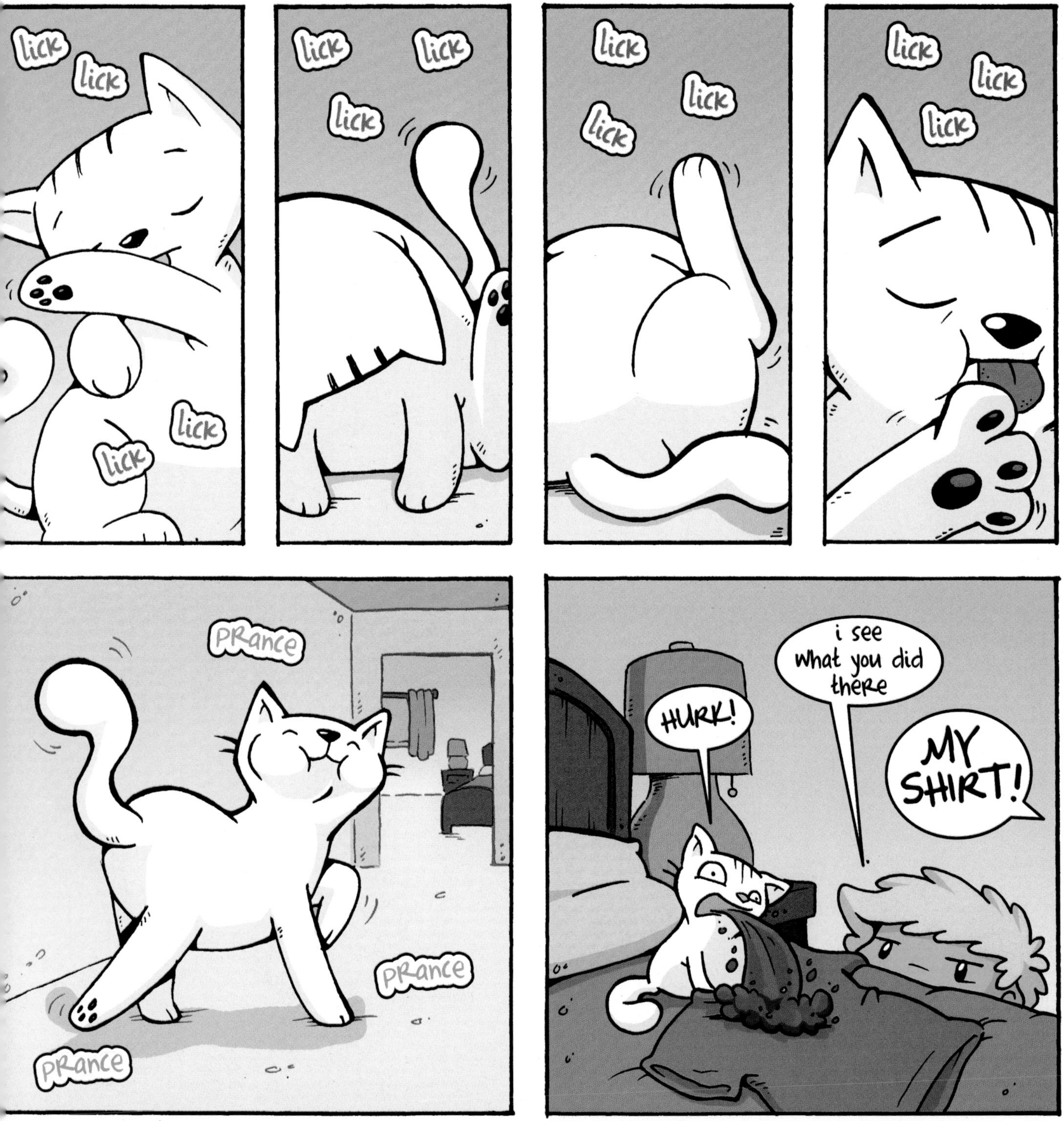
lick
lick
lick
lick
lick
lick
lick
lick
lick
lick
lick
lick
lick
PRance
PRance
PRance
HURK!
i see what you did there
MY SHIRT!

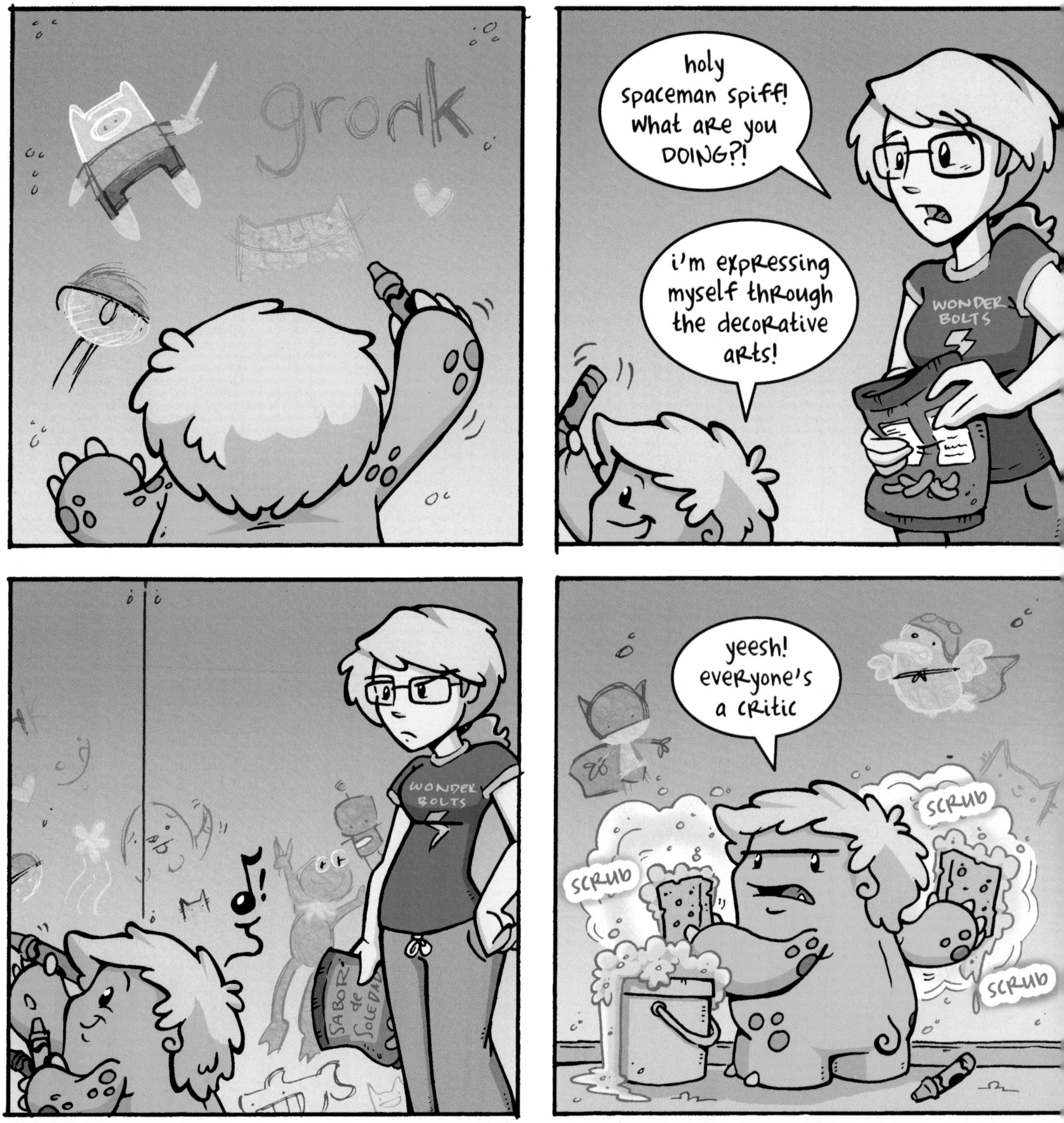
gronk
holy spaceman spiff! What are you DOING?!
i'm expressing myself through the decorative arts!
WONDER BOLTS
SABOR de SOLEDAD
yeesh! everyone's a critic
SCRUB
SCRUB
SCRUB

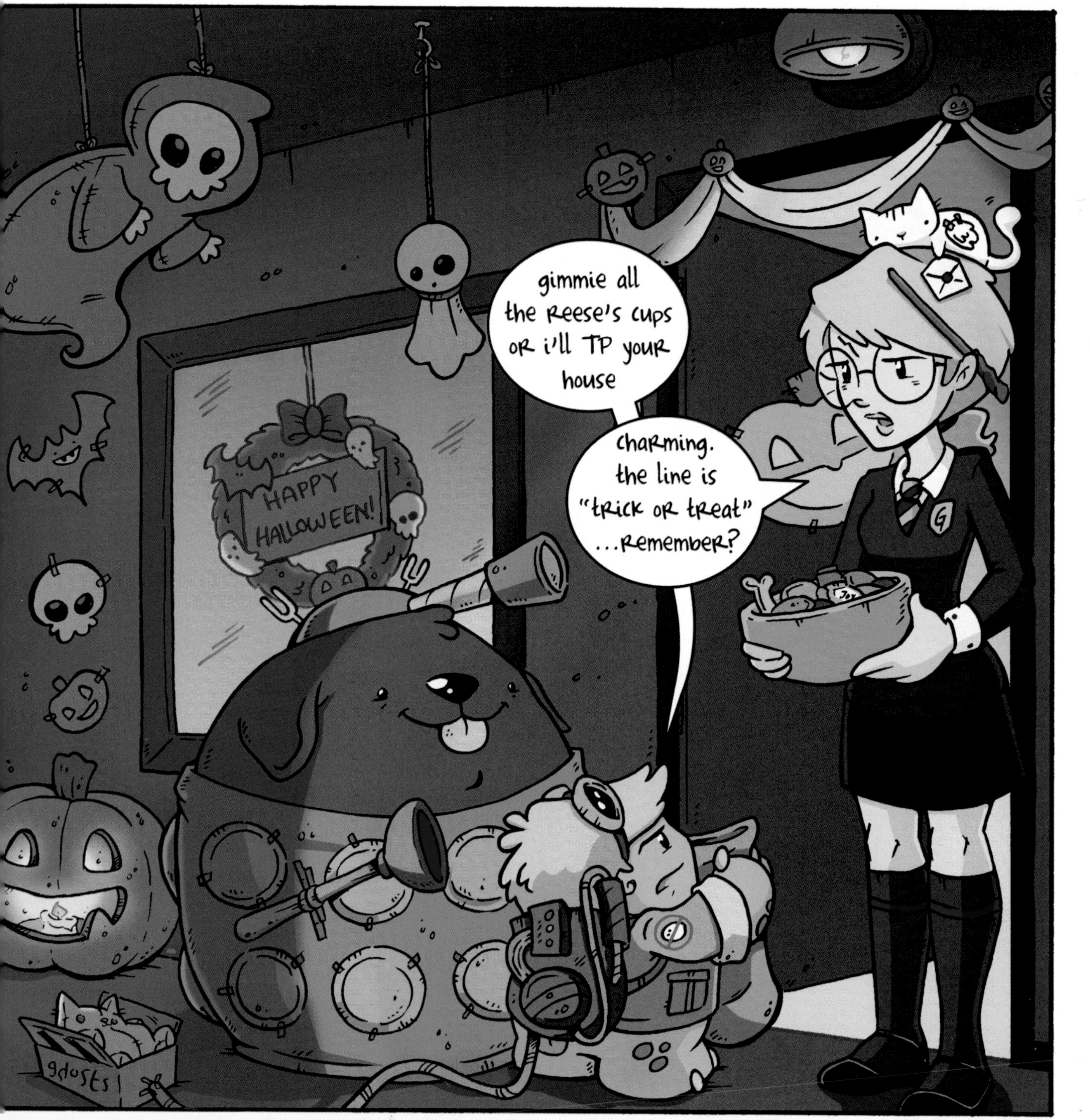
HAPPY HALLOWEEN!
gimmie all the Reese's cups or i'll TP your house
charming. the line is "trick or treat" ...remember?
ghosts

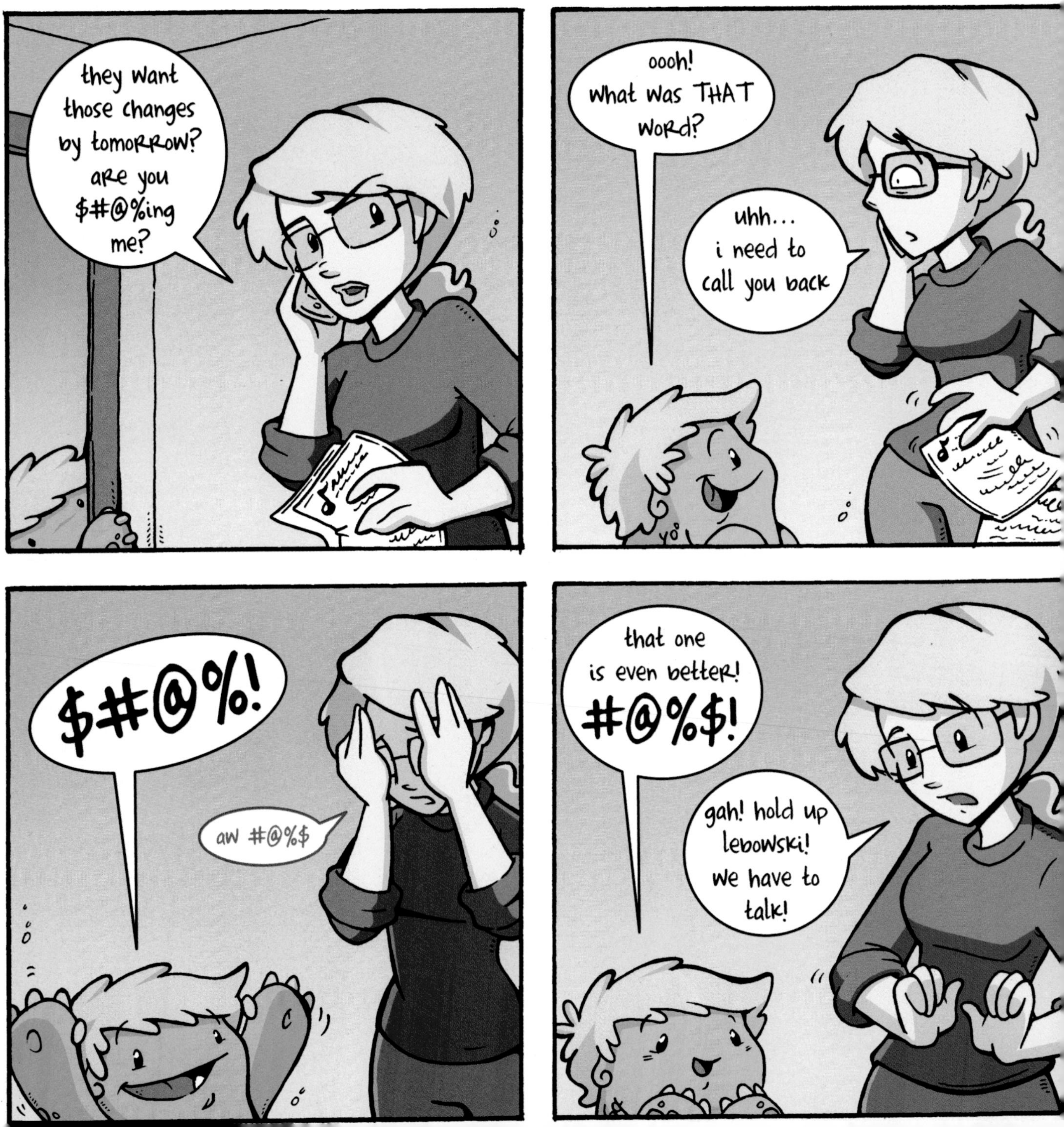
they want those changes by tomorrow? are you $#@%ing me?
oooh! What was THAT word?
uhh... i need to call you back
$#@%!
aw #@%$
that one is even better! #@%$!
gah! hold up lebowski! we have to talk!

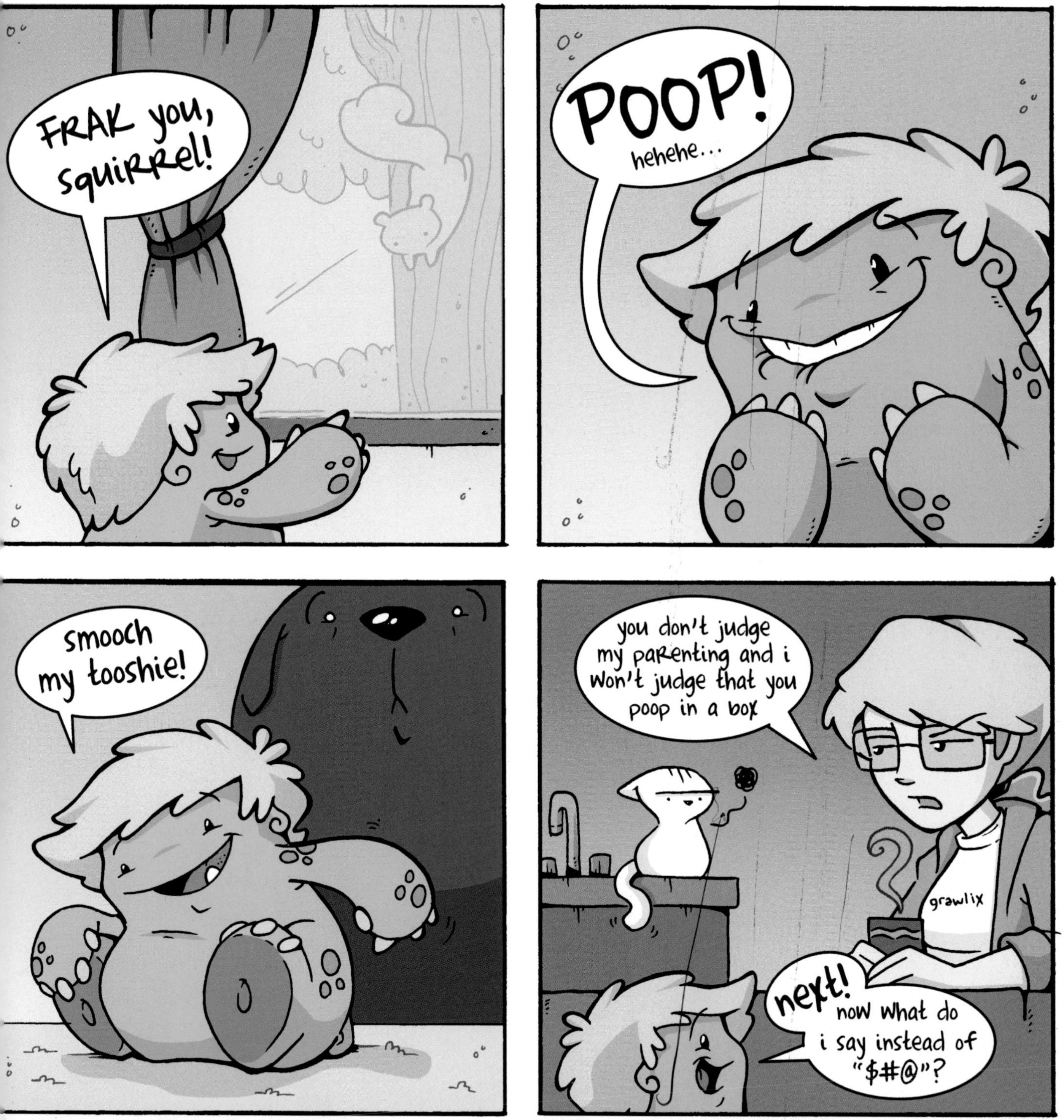
FRAK you, squirrel!
POOP!
hehehe...
smooch my tooshie!
you don't judge my parenting and i won't judge that you poop in a box
grawlix
next!
now what do i say instead of "$#@"?

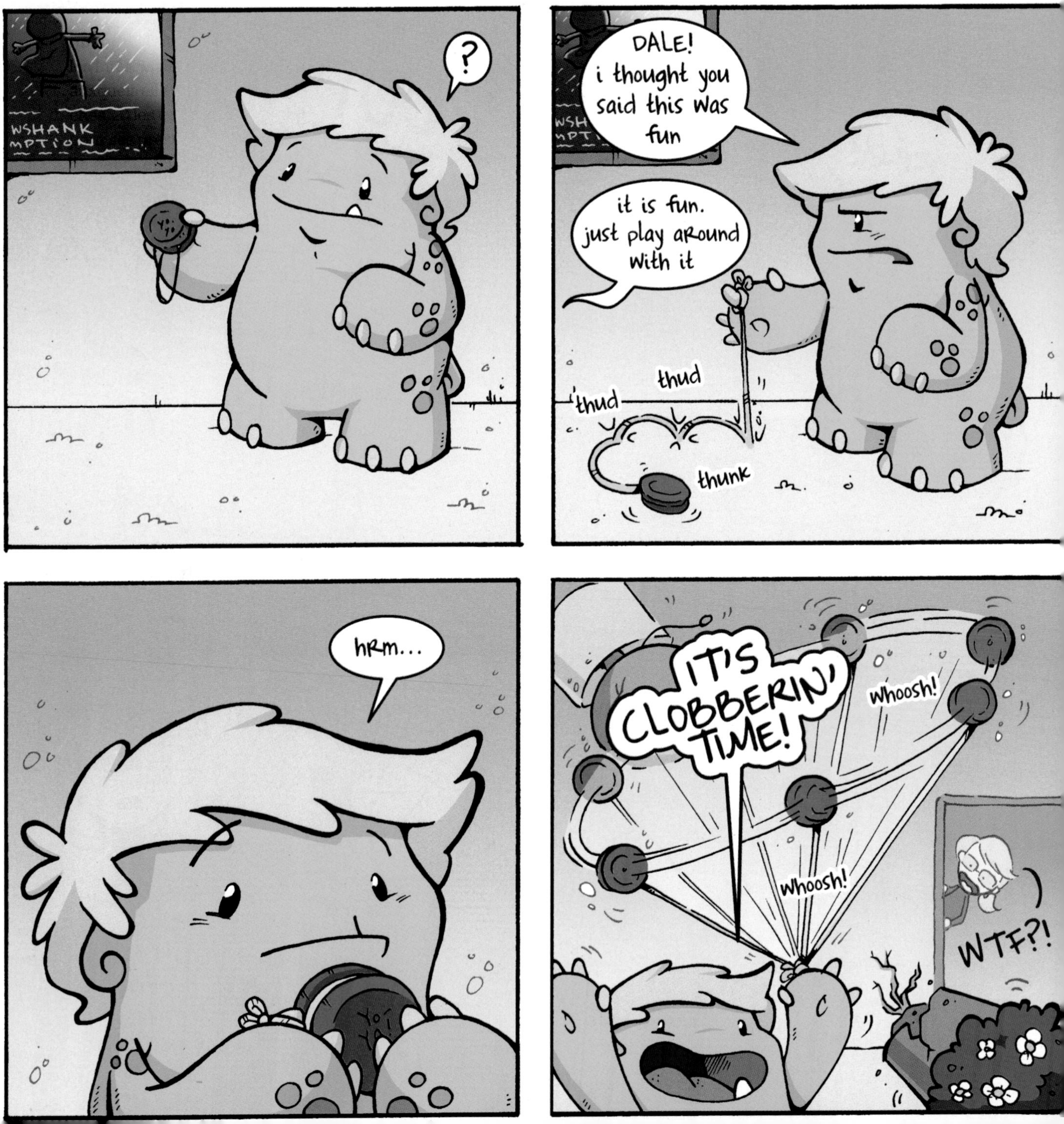
?
DALE!
i thought you said this was fun
it is fun.
just play around with it
thud
thud
thud
thunk
hrm...
IT'S CLOBBERIN' TIME!
whoosh!
whoosh!
WTF?!

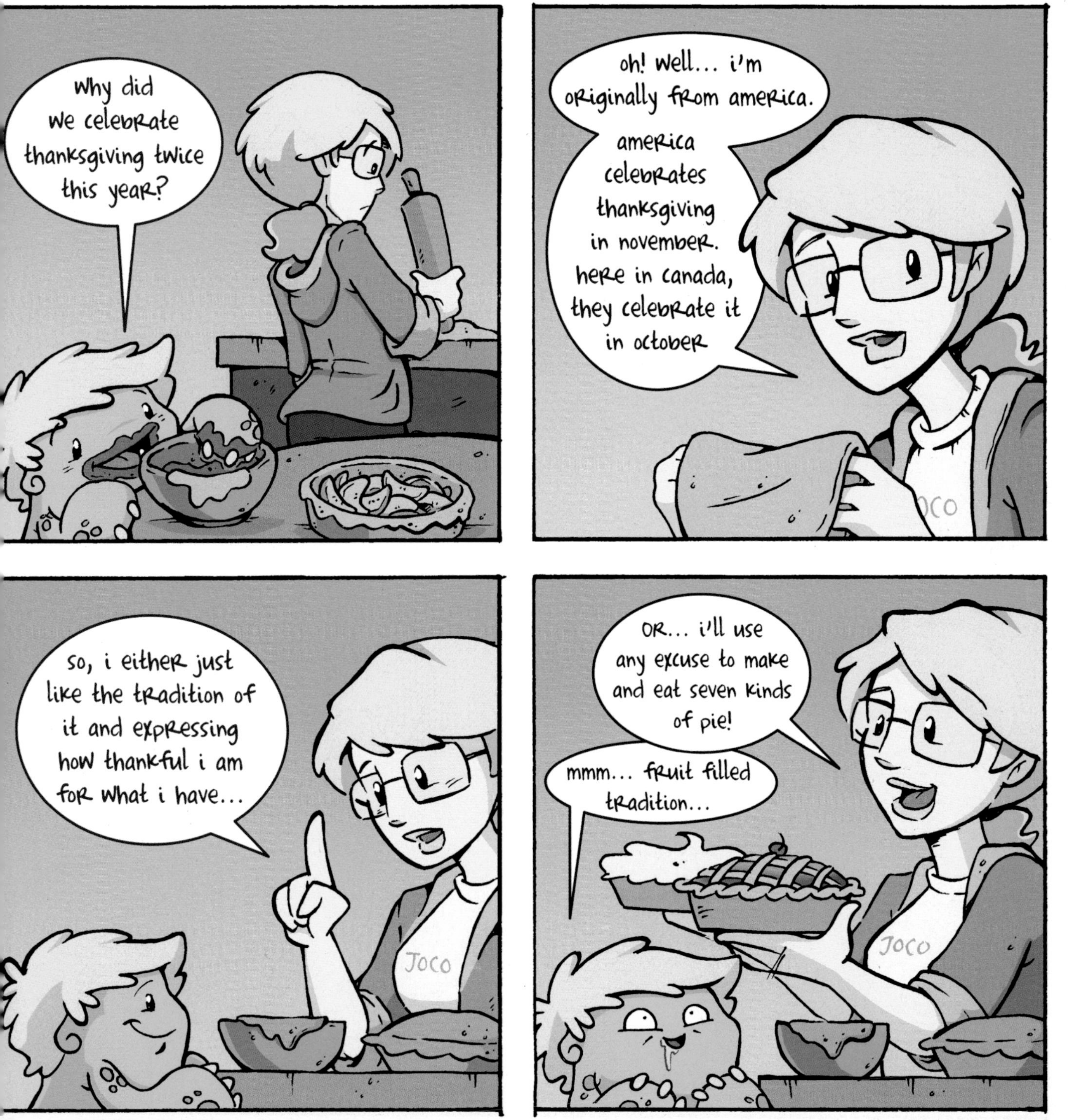
why did we celebrate thanksgiving twice this year?
oh! well... i'm originally from america.
america celebrates thanksgiving in november. here in canada, they celebrate it in october
so, i either just like the tradition of it and expressing how thankful i am for what i have...
or... i'll use any excuse to make and eat seven kinds of pie!
mmm... fruit filled tradition...
JOCO

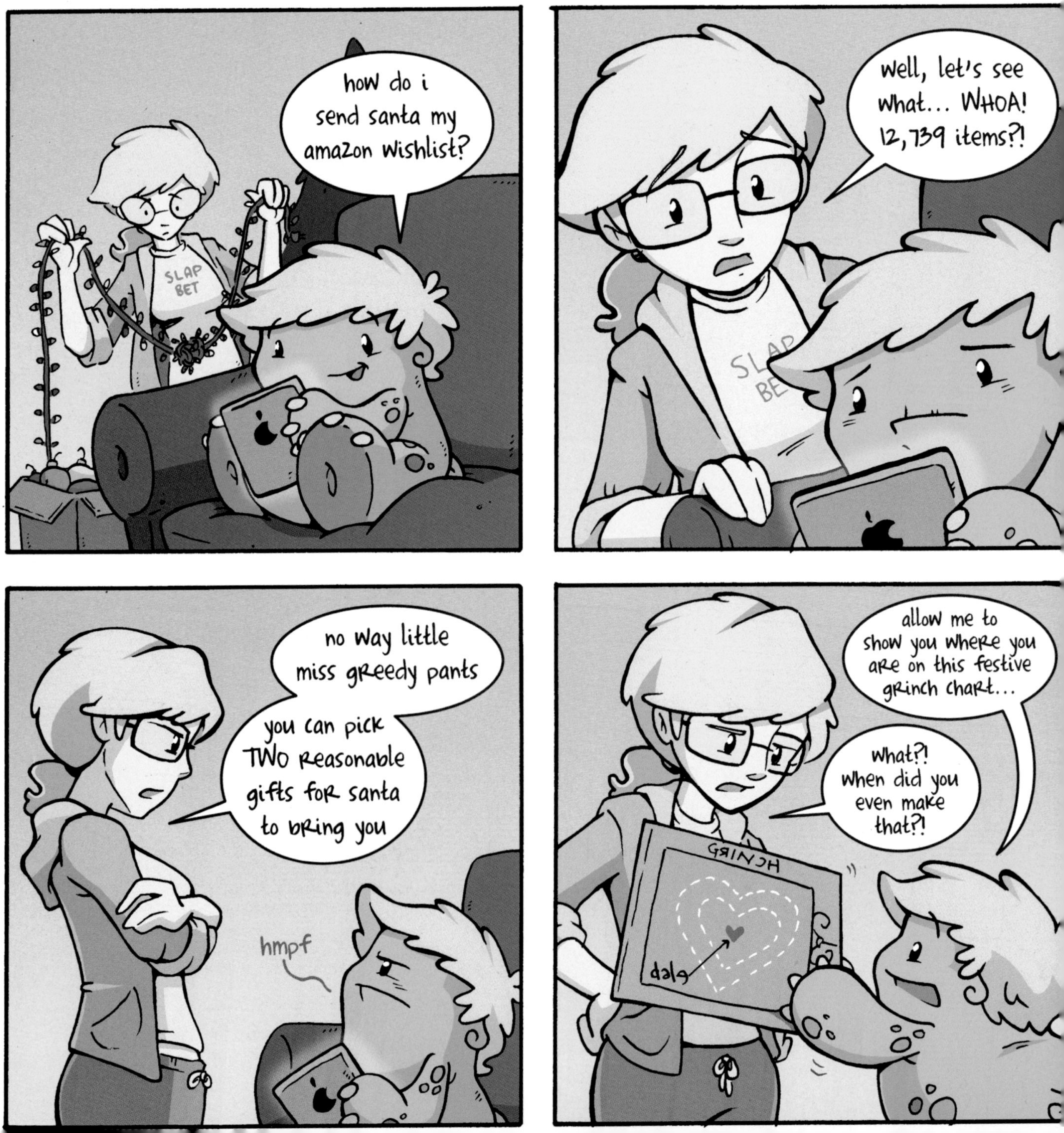
how do i send santa my amazon wishlist?
SLAP BET
well, let's see what... WHOA! 12,739 items?!
SLAP BET
no way little miss greedy pants
you can pick TWO reasonable gifts for santa to bring you
hmpf
allow me to show you where you are on this festive grinch chart...
what?! when did you even make that?!
GRINCH
dalg

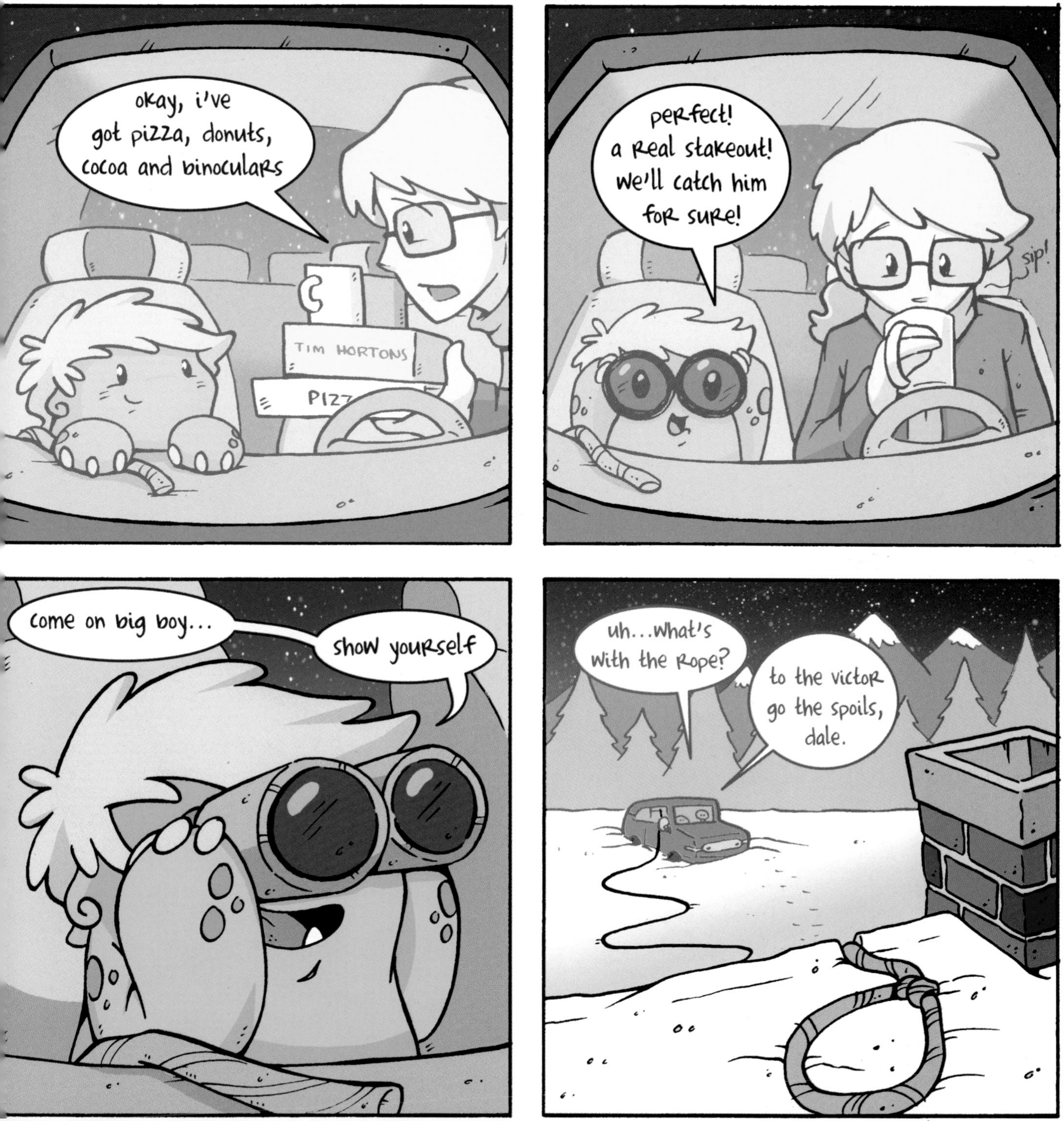
okay, i've got pizza, donuts, cocoa and binoculars
TIM HORTONS
PIZ
perfect! a real stakeout! we'll catch him for sure!
sip!
come on big boy...
show yourself
uh...what's with the rope?
to the victor go the spoils, dale.

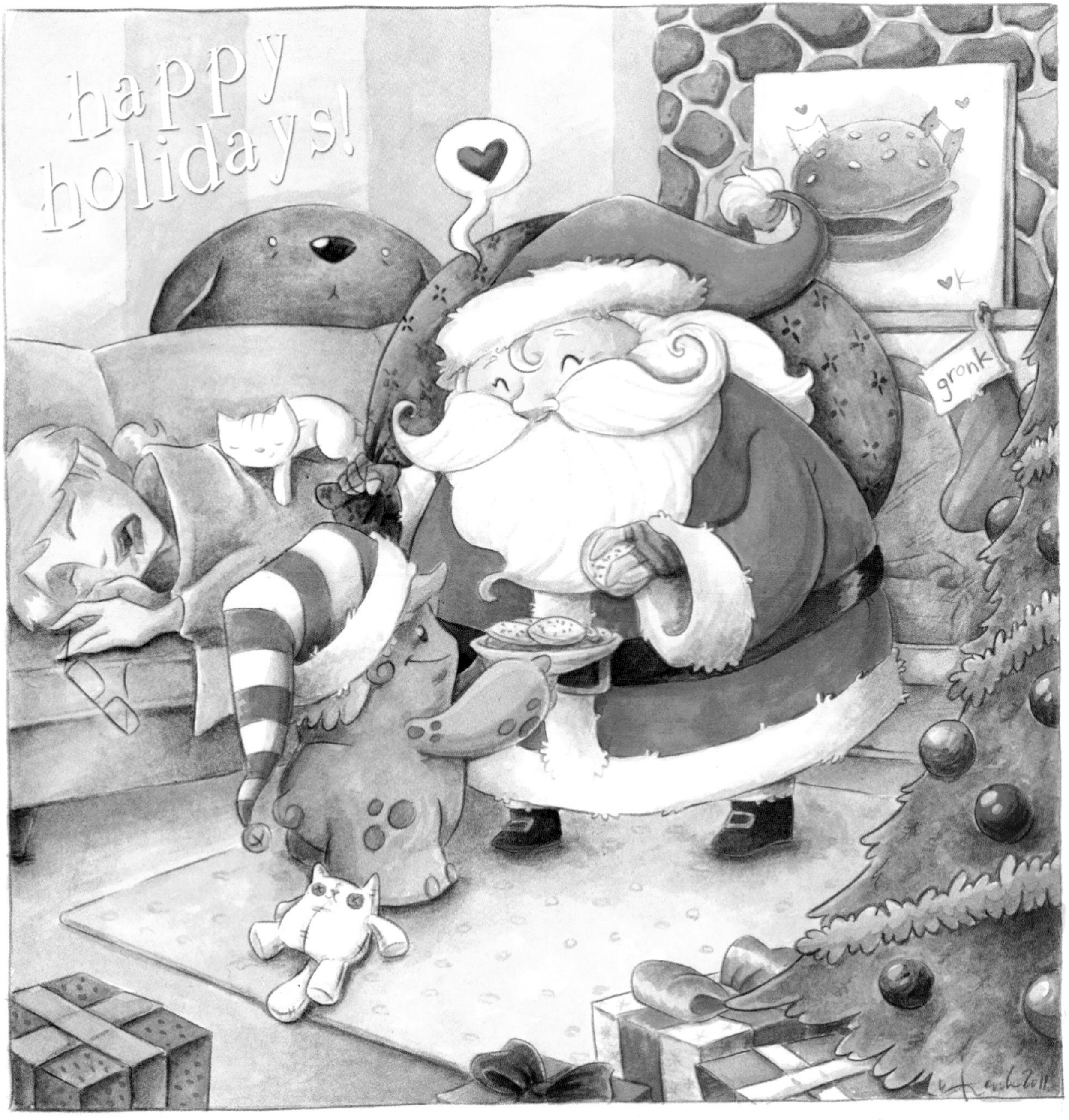
happy holidays!
gronk

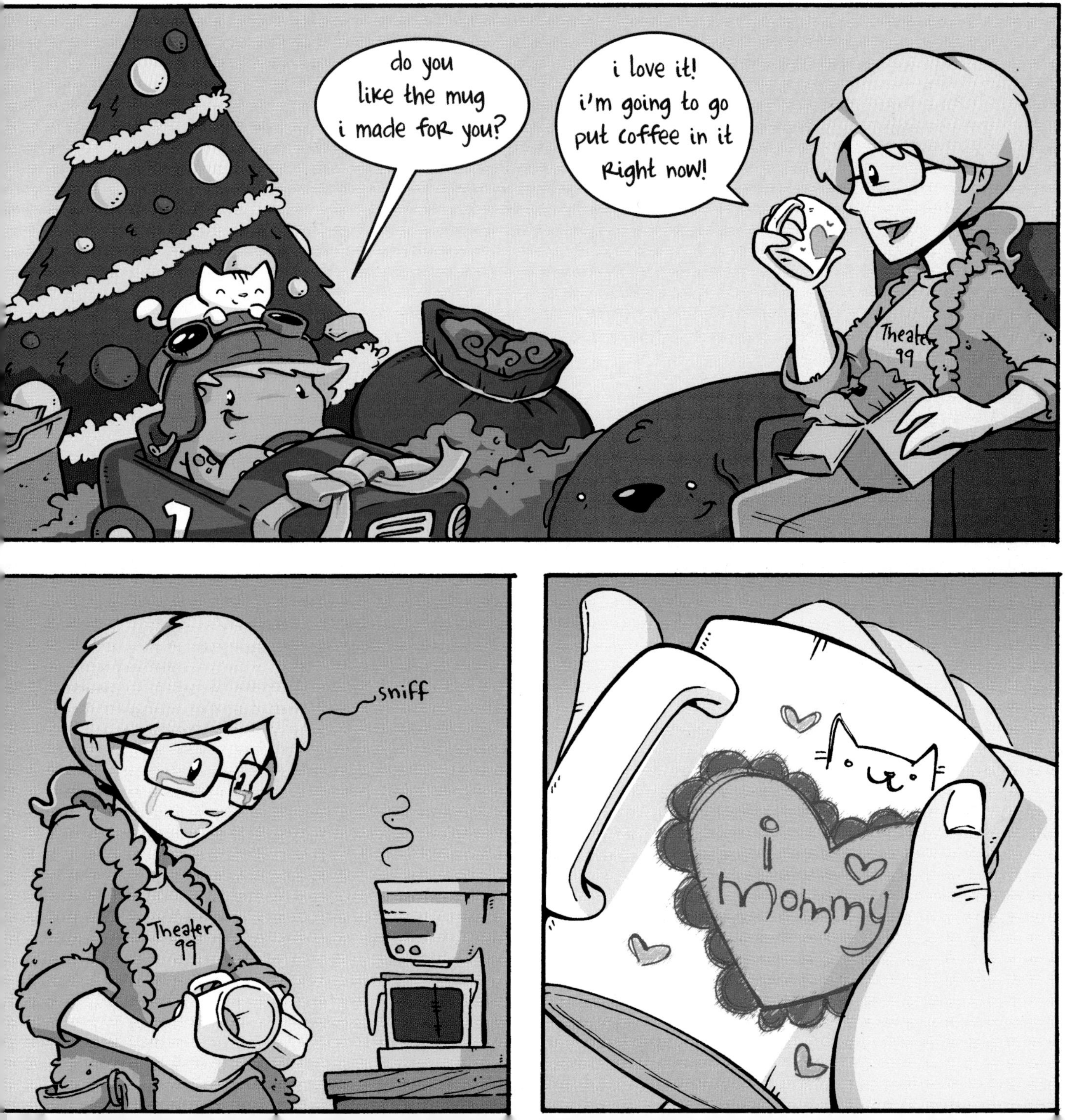
do you like the mug i made for you?
i love it! i'm going to go put coffee in it right now!
Theater 99
sniff
Theater 99
i mommy

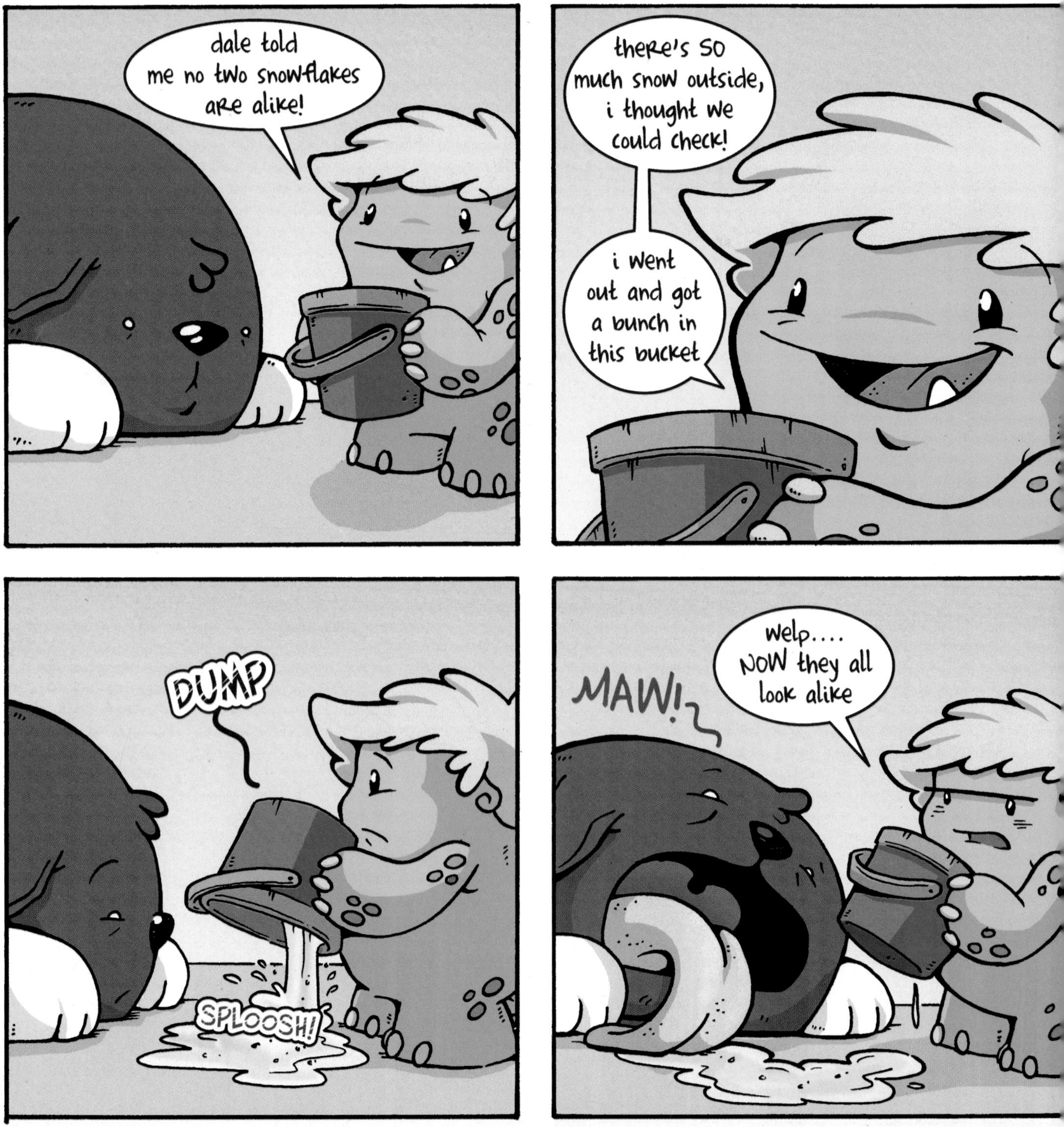
dale told me no two snowflakes are alike!
there's so much snow outside, i thought we could check!
i went out and got a bunch in this bucket
DUMP
SPLOOSH!
MAW!
welp.... NOW they all look alike

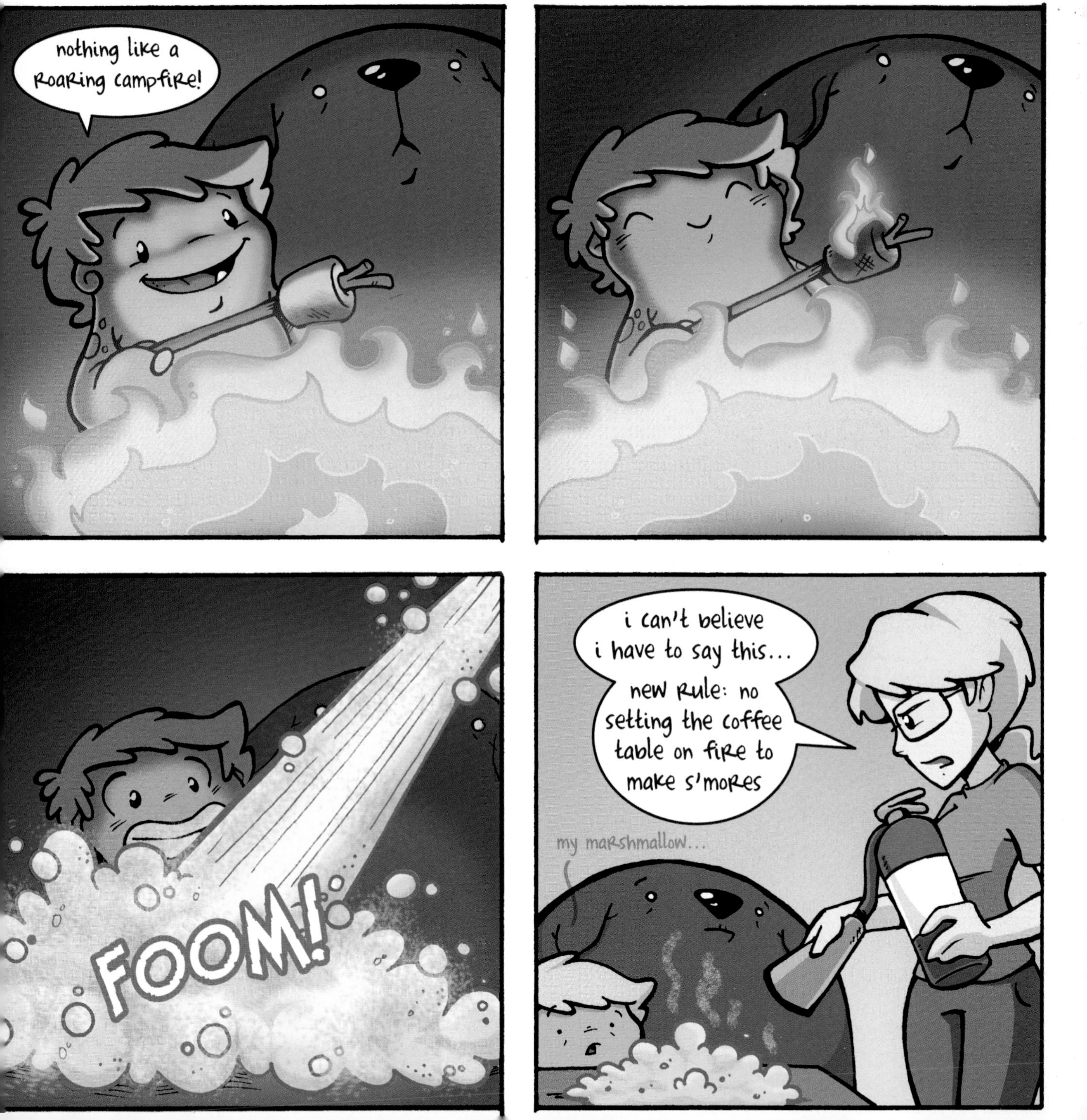
nothing like a roaring campfire!
FOOM!
i can't believe i have to say this...
new rule: no setting the coffee table on fire to make s'mores
my marshmallow...

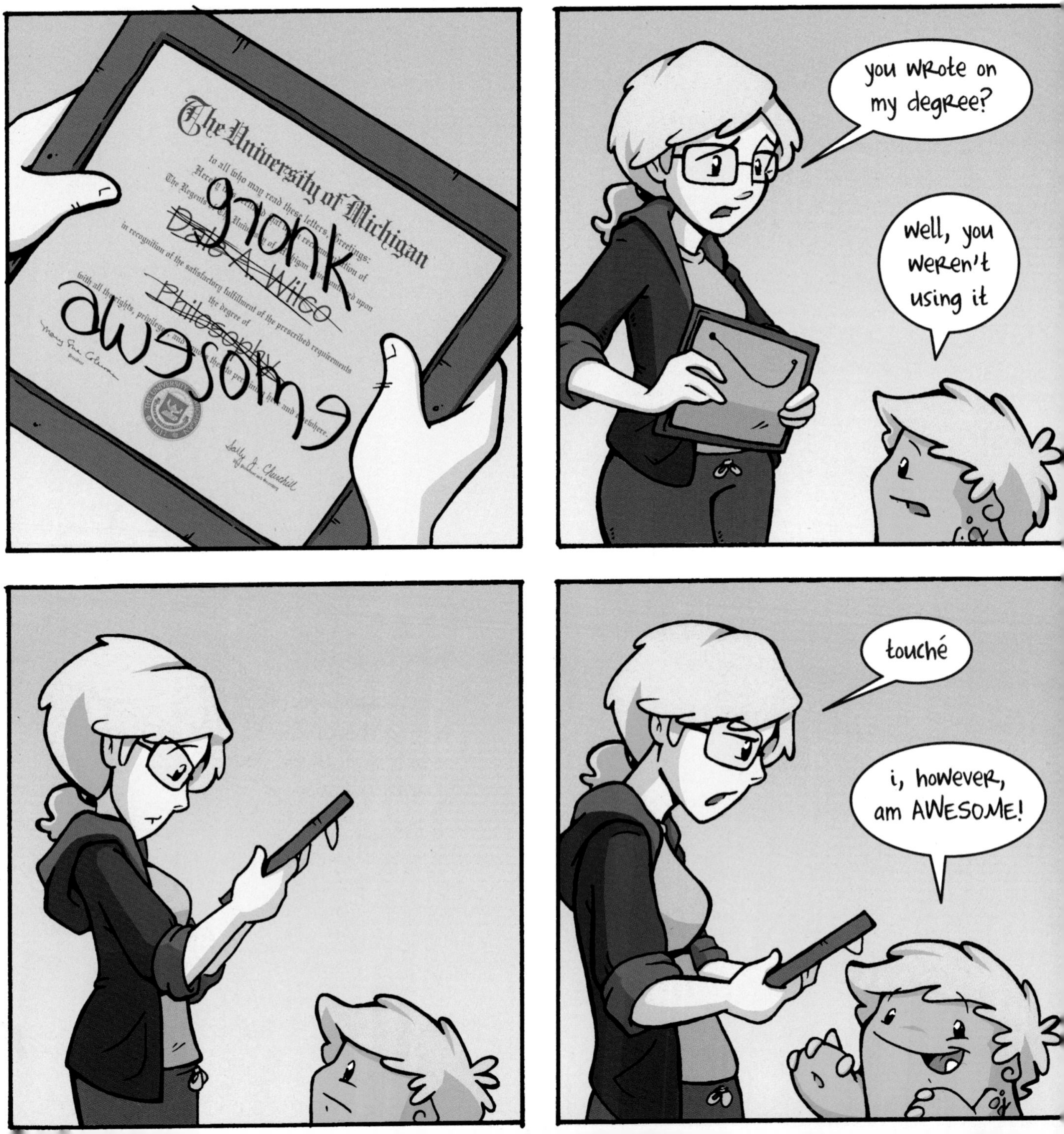
The University of Michigan
gronk
awesome
you wrote on my degree?
well, you weren't using it
touché
i, however, am AWESOME!

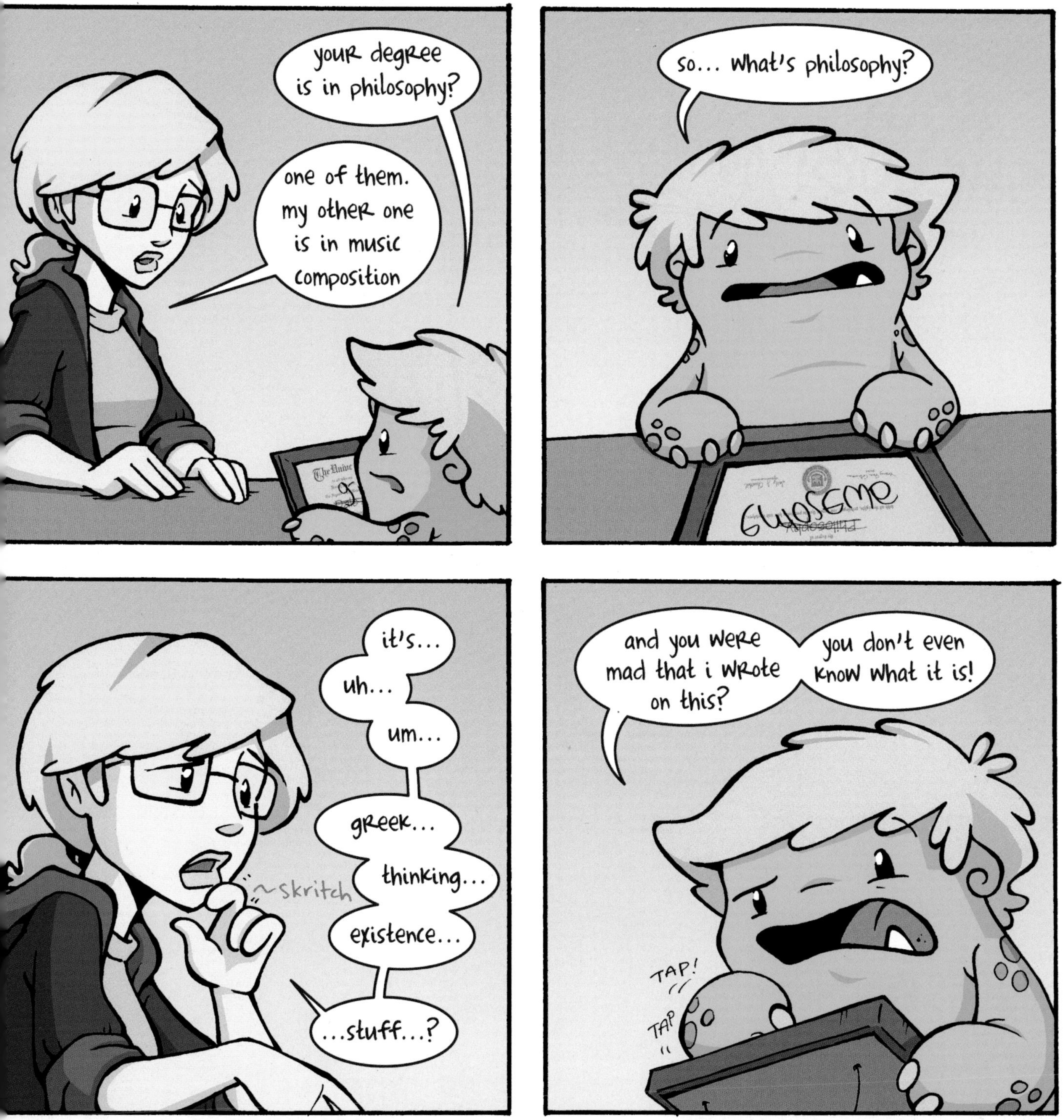
your degree is in philosophy?
one of them. my other one is in music composition
so... what's philosophy?
it's...
uh...
um...
greek...
thinking...
existence...
...stuff...?
~skritch
and you were mad that i wrote on this?
you don't even know what it is!
TAP!
TAP

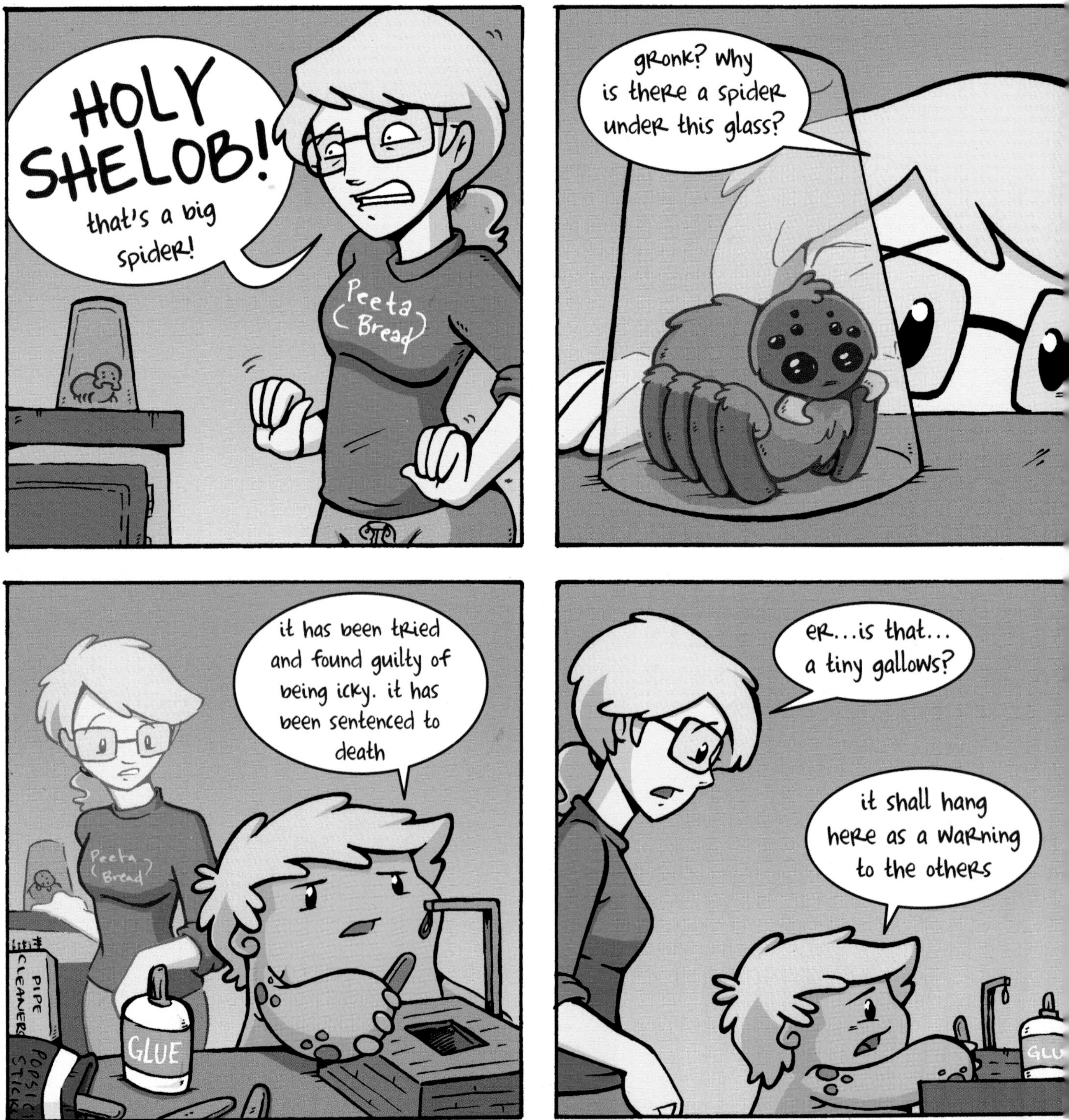
HOLY SHELOB! that's a big spider!
Peeta (Bread)
gRonk? why is there a spider under this glass?
it has been tried and found guilty of being icky. it has been sentenced to death
Peeta (Bread)
PIPE CLEANERS
POPSICLE STICKS
GLUE
eR...is that... a tiny gallows?
it shall hang here as a warning to the others

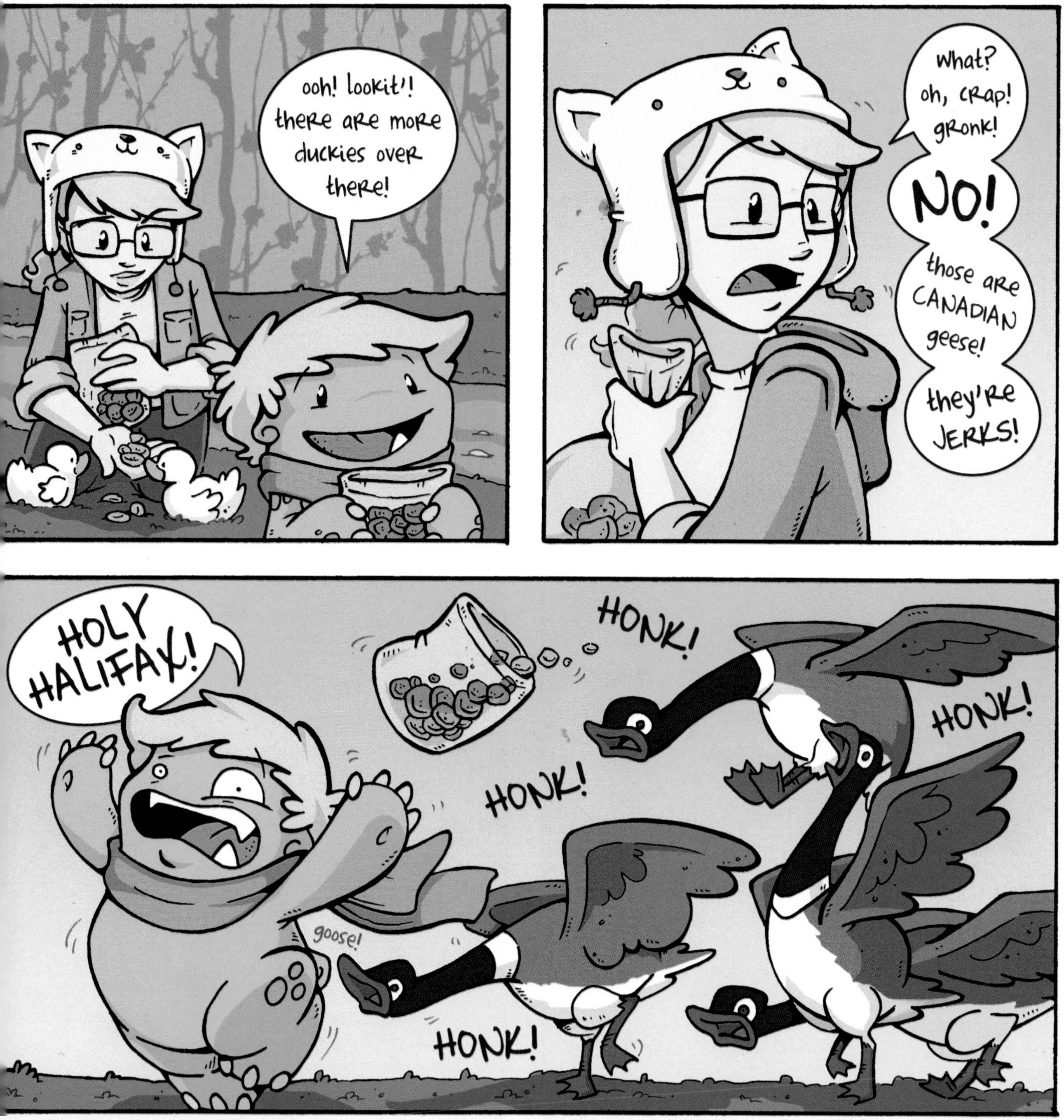

ooh! lookit'! there are more duckies over there!
what? oh, crap! gronk!
NO!
those are CANADIAN geese!
they're JERKS!
HOLY HALIFAX!
HONK!
HONK!
HONK!
goose!
HONK!

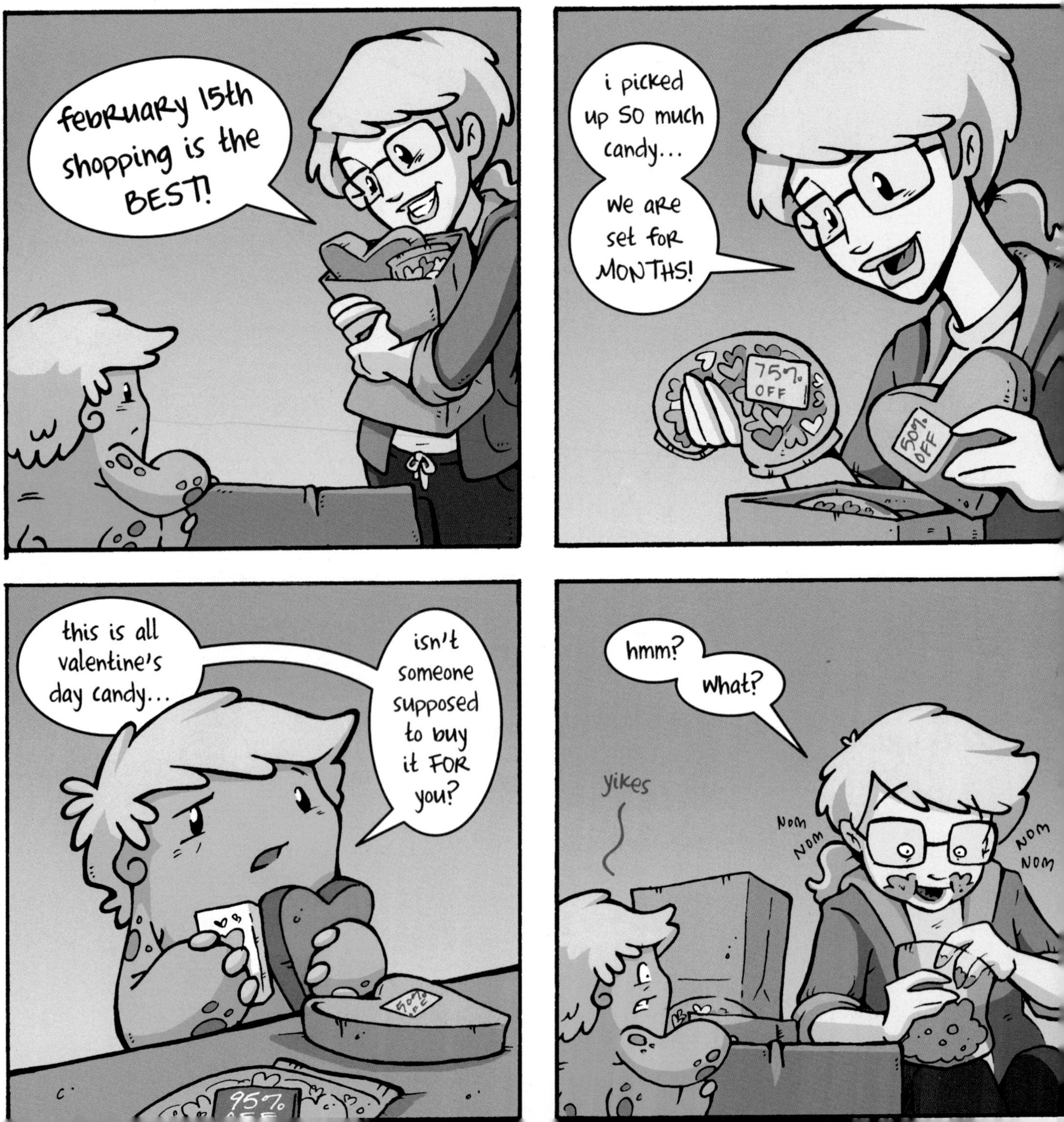
february 15th shopping is the BEST!
i picked up SO much candy...
we are set for MONTHS!
75% OFF
50% OFF
this is all valentine's day candy...
isn't someone supposed to buy it FOR you?
95%
hmm?
what?
yikes
NOM NOM
NOM NOM

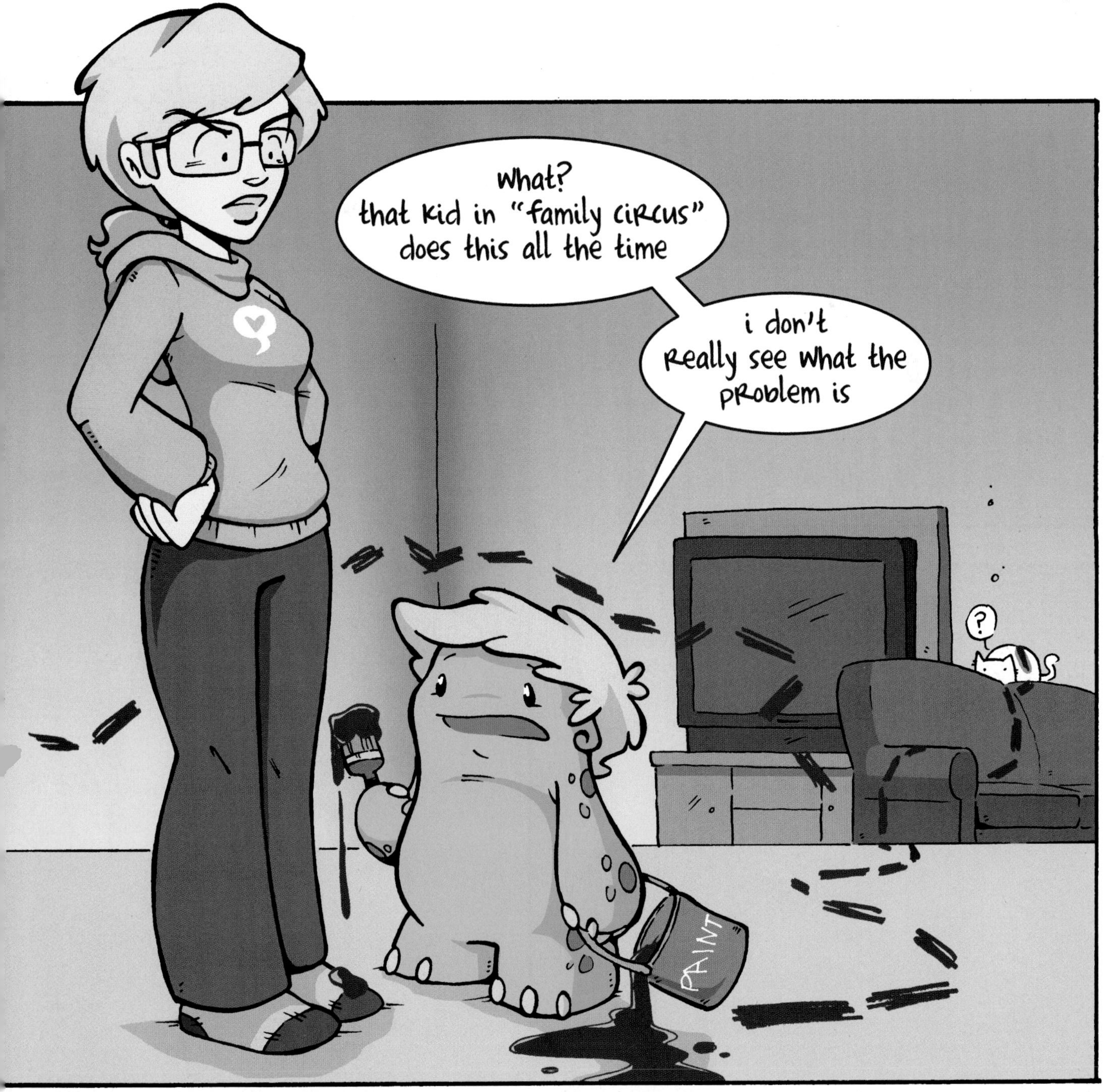
what?
that kid in "family circus"
does this all the time
i don't
really see what the
problem is
?
PAINT

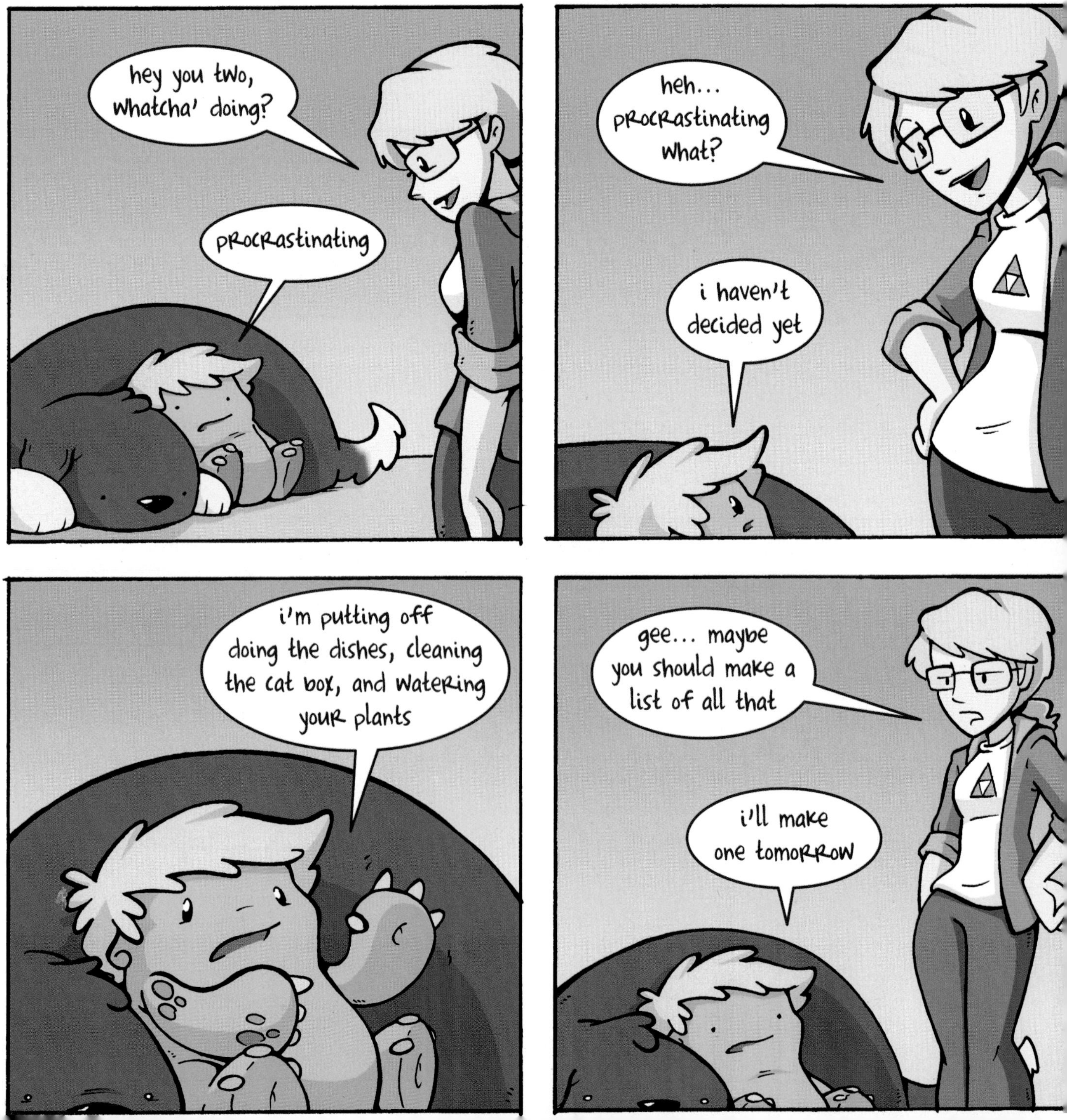
hey you two, whatcha' doing?
procrastinating
heh... procrastinating what?
i haven't decided yet
i'm putting off doing the dishes, cleaning the cat box, and watering your plants
gee... maybe you should make a list of all that
i'll make one tomorrow

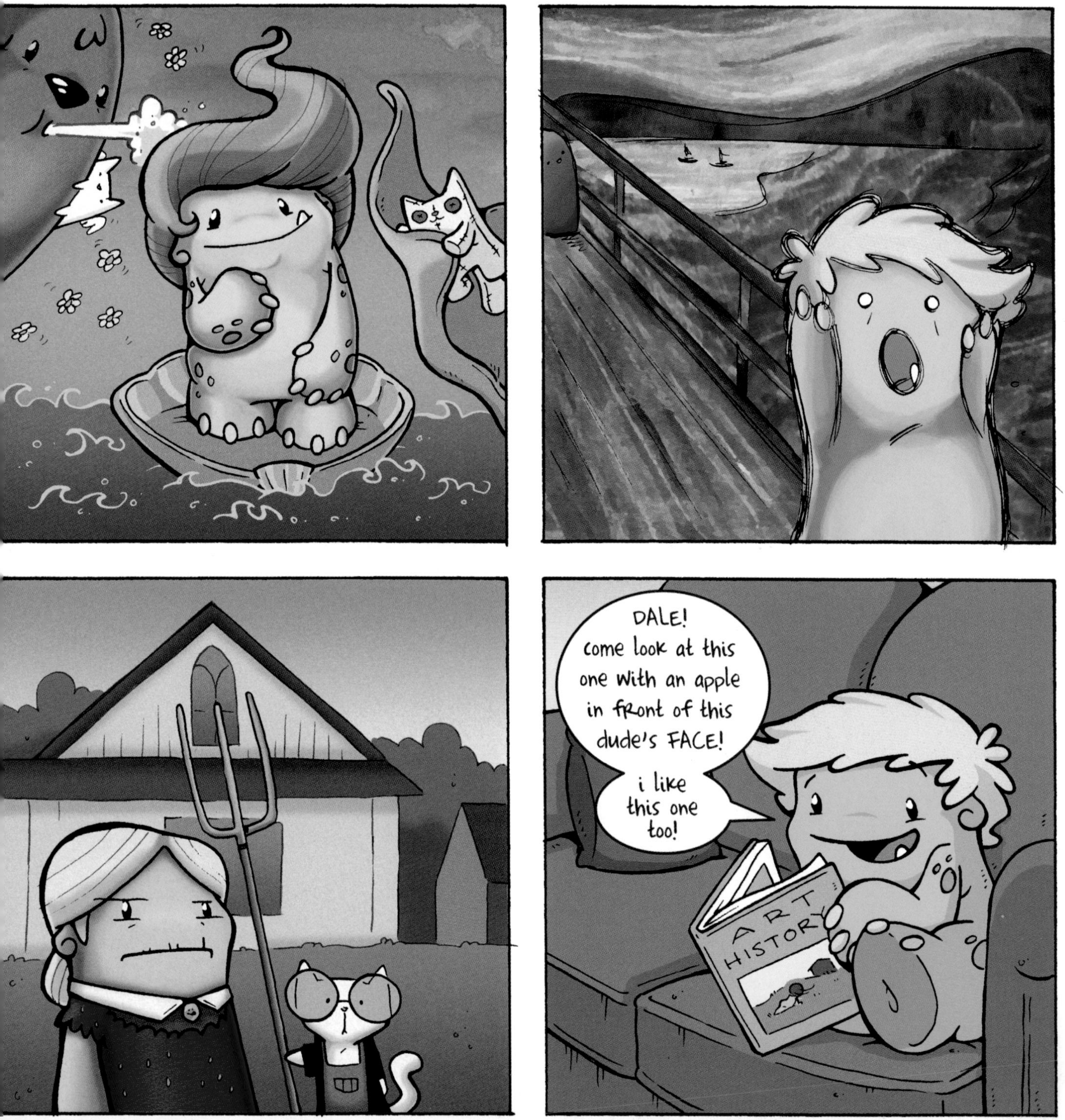

DALE! come look at this one with an apple in front of this dude's FACE!
i like this one too!
ART HISTORY

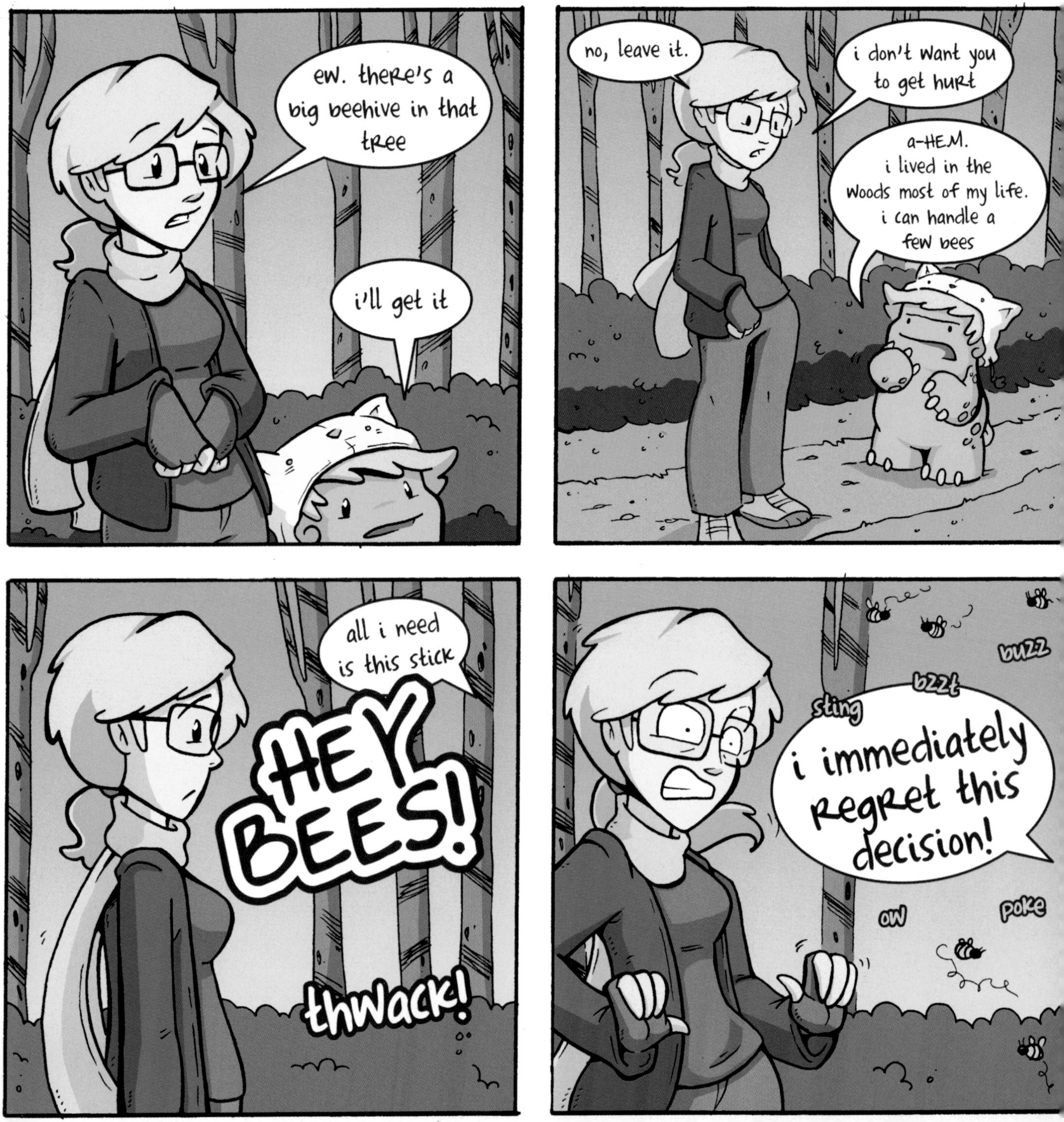
ew. there's a big beehive in that tree
i'll get it
no, leave it.
i don't want you to get hurt
a-HEM. i lived in the woods most of my life. i can handle a few bees
all i need is this stick
HEY BEES!
thwack!
buzz
bzzt
sting
i immediately regret this decision!
ow
poke

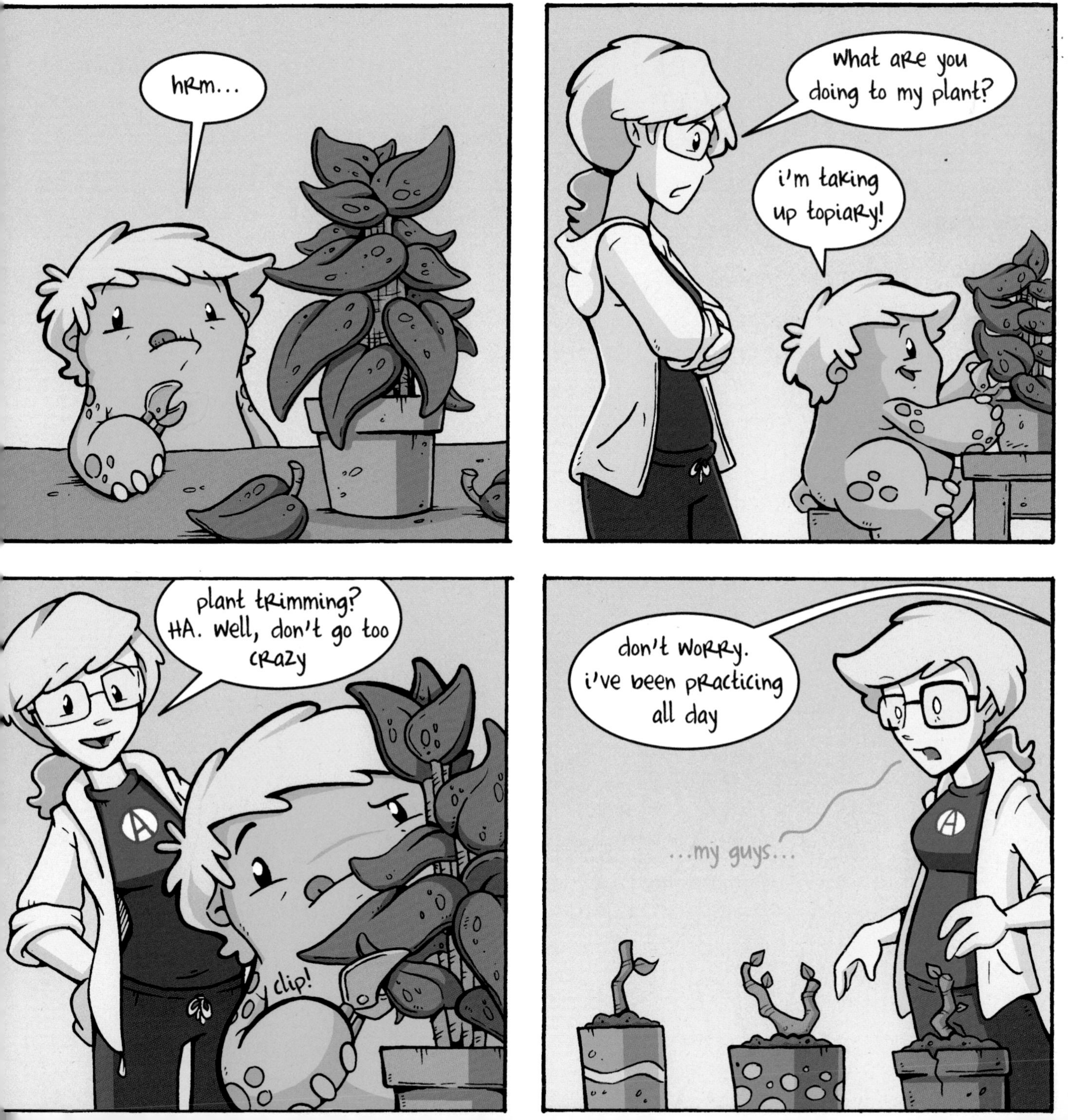
hrm...
What are you doing to my plant?
i'm taking up topiary!
plant trimming? HA. Well, don't go too crazy
clip!
don't worry. i've been practicing all day
...my guys...

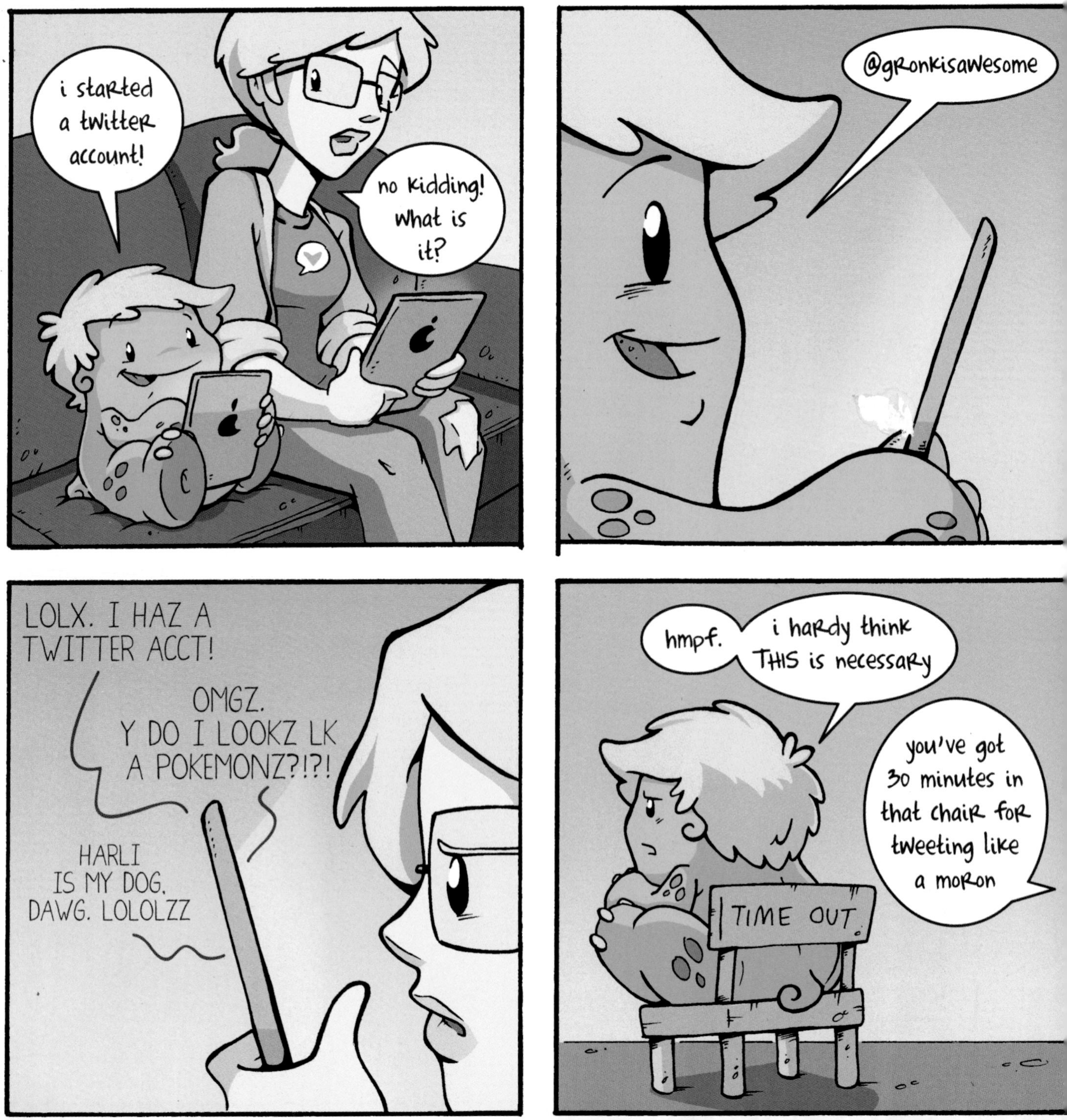
i started a twitter account!
no kidding! what is it?
@gronkisawesome
LOLX. I HAZ A TWITTER ACCT!
OMGZ. Y DO I LOOKZ LK A POKEMONZ?!?!
HARLI IS MY DOG. DAWG. LOLOLZZ
hmpf.
i hardy think THIS is necessary
you've got 30 minutes in that chair for tweeting like a moron
TIME OUT

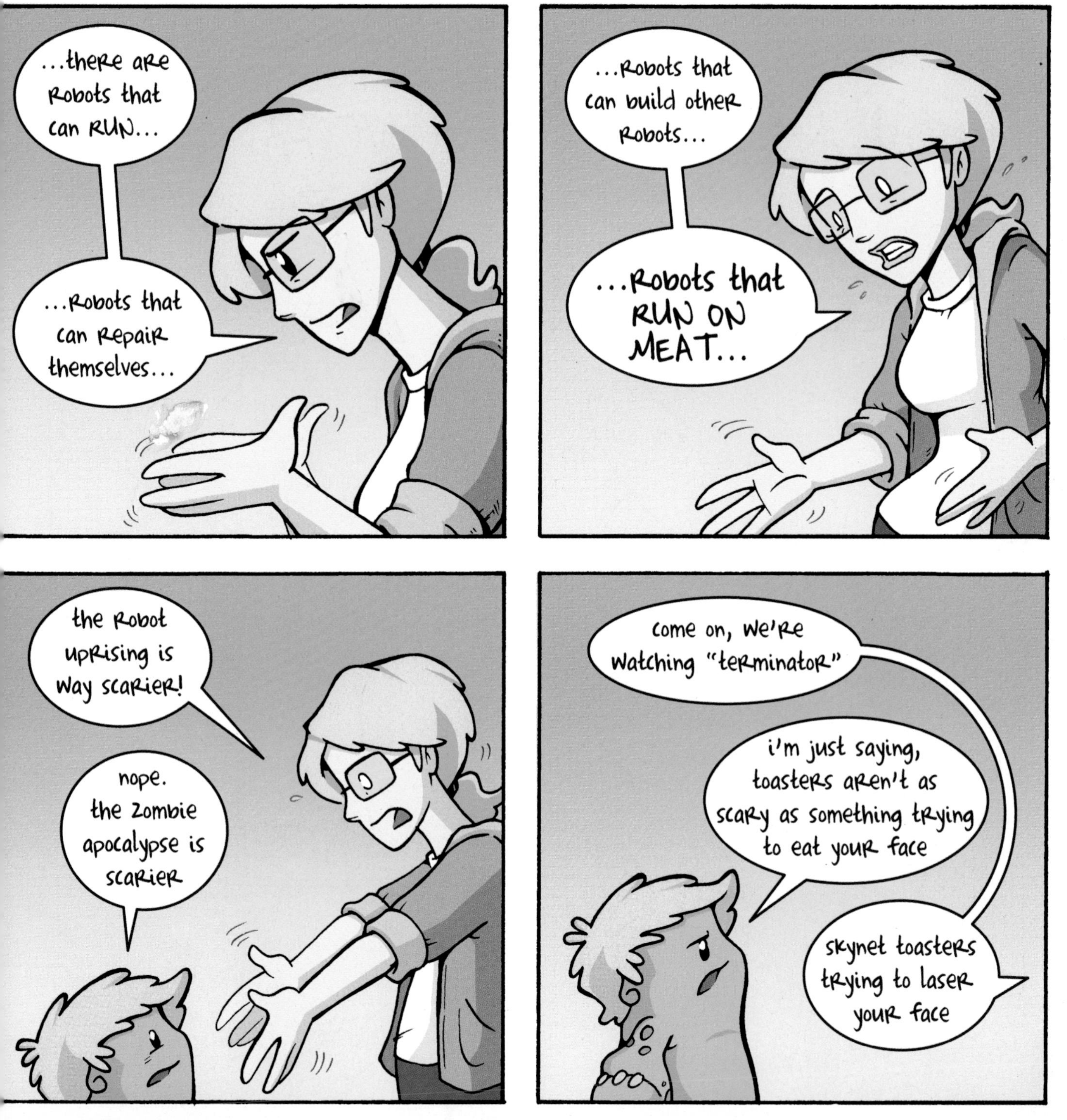
...there are robots that can RUN...
...robots that can repair themselves...
...robots that can build other robots...
...robots that RUN ON MEAT...
the robot uprising is way scarier!
nope. the zombie apocalypse is scarier
come on, we're watching "terminator"
i'm just saying, toasters aren't as scary as something trying to eat your face
skynet toasters trying to laser your face

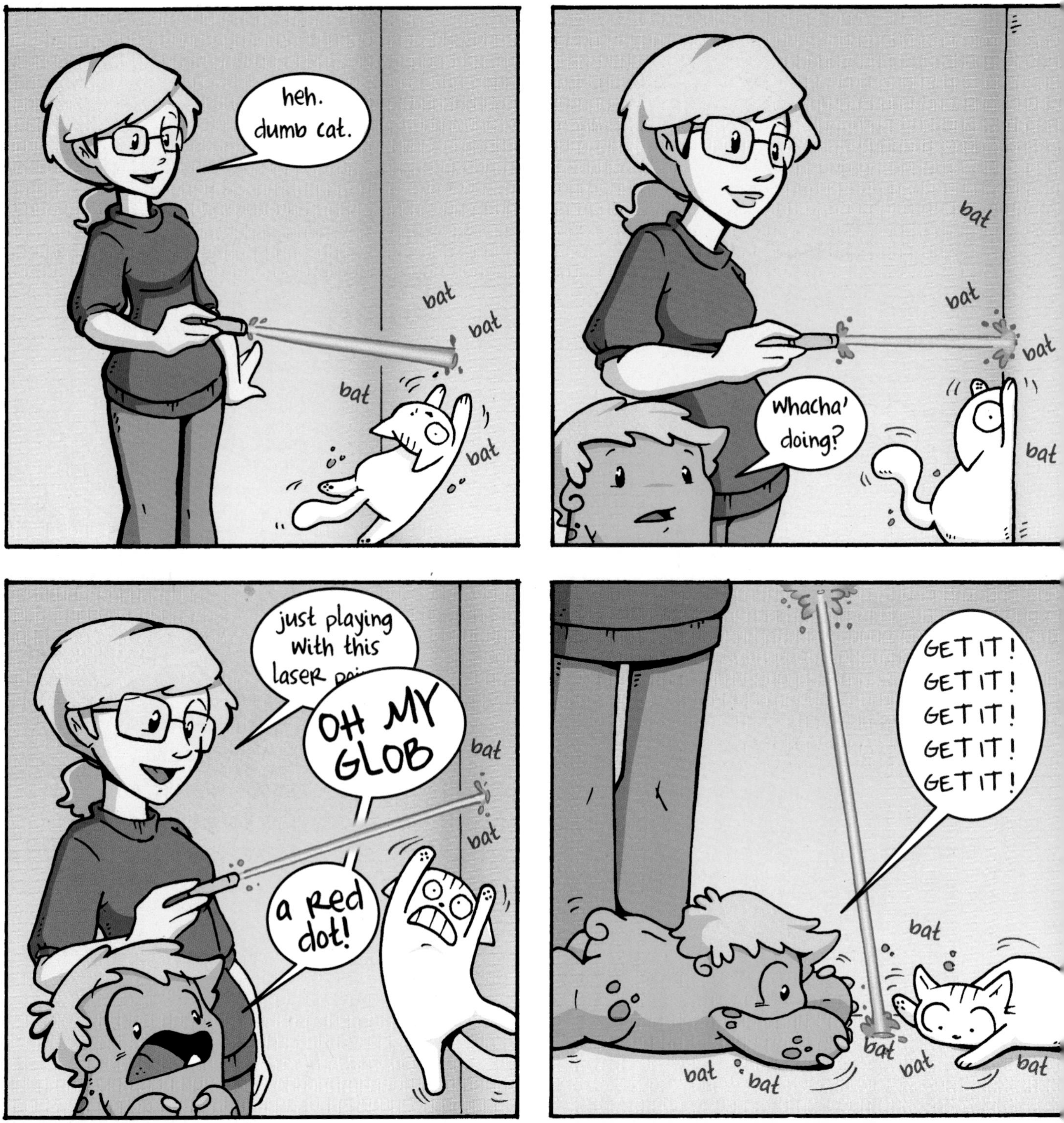
heh.
dumb cat.
bat
bat
bat
bat
bat
bat
bat
bat
Whacha' doing?
just playing with this laser
OH MY GLOB
a red dot!
bat
bat
GET IT!
GET IT!
GET IT!
GET IT!
GET IT!
bat
bat
bat
bat
bat
bat

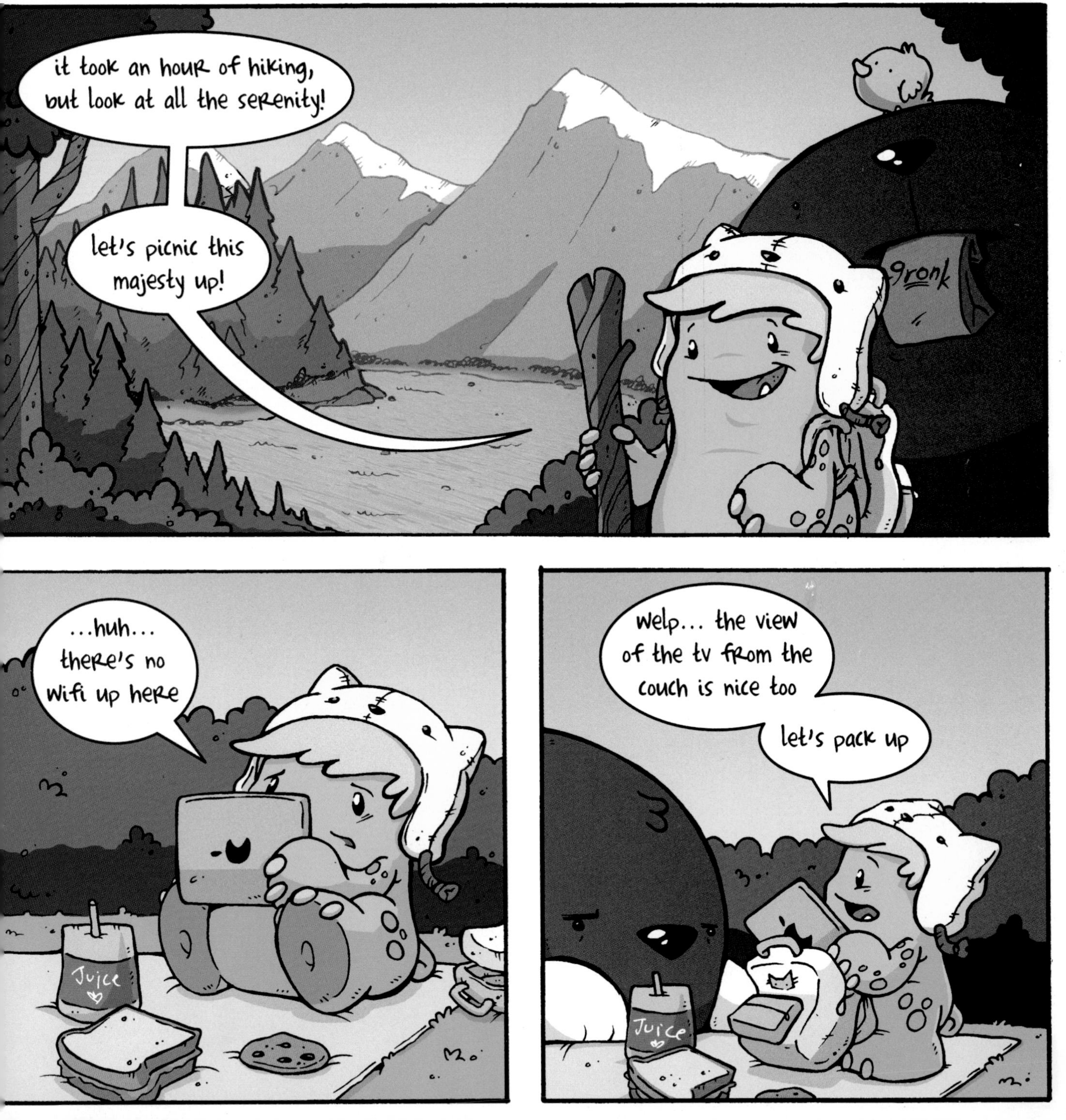
it took an hour of hiking, but look at all the serenity!
let's picnic this majesty up!
gronk
...huh... there's no wifi up here
Juice
welp... the view of the tv from the couch is nice too
let's pack up
Juice

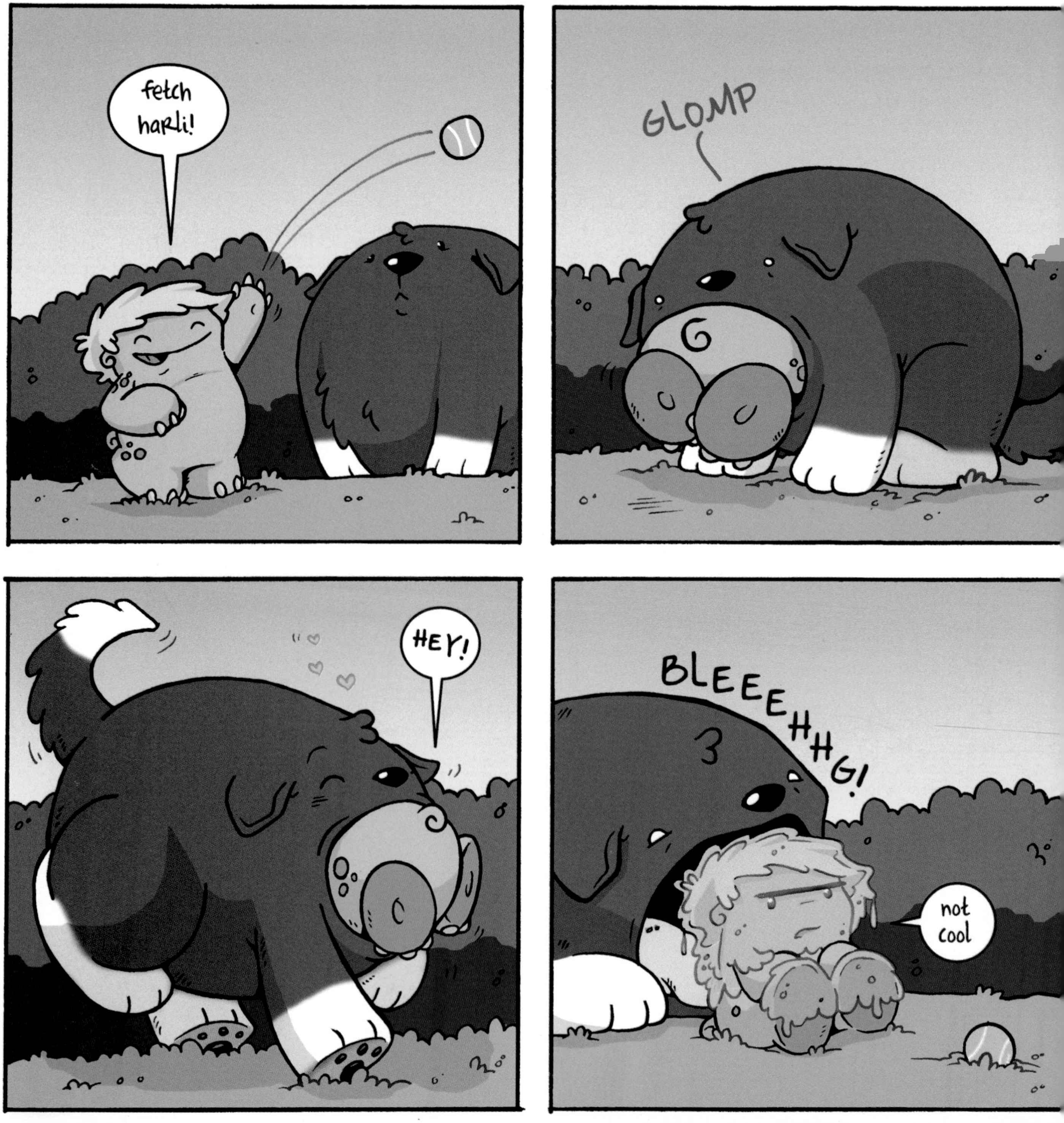
fetch harli!
GLOMP
HEY!
BLEEEHHHG!
not cool

art by david petersen

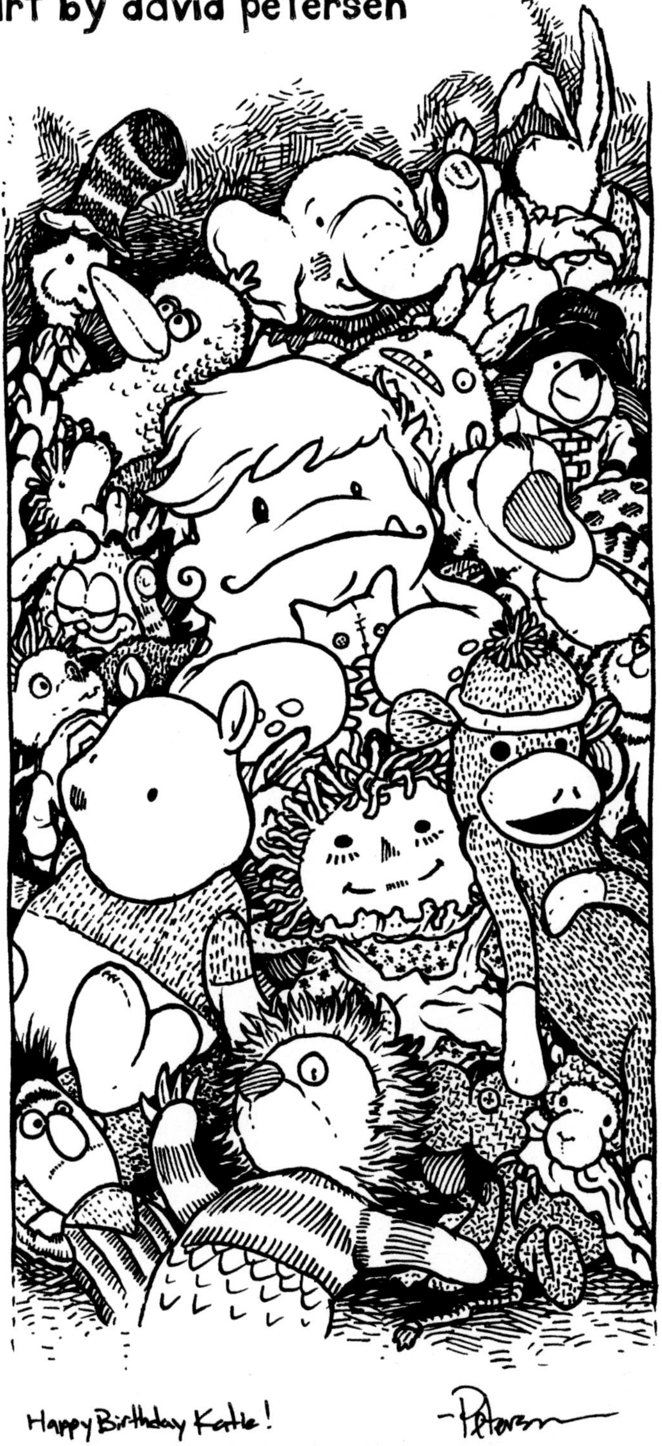
Happy Birthday Katie!
-Petersen

art by jeremy bastian

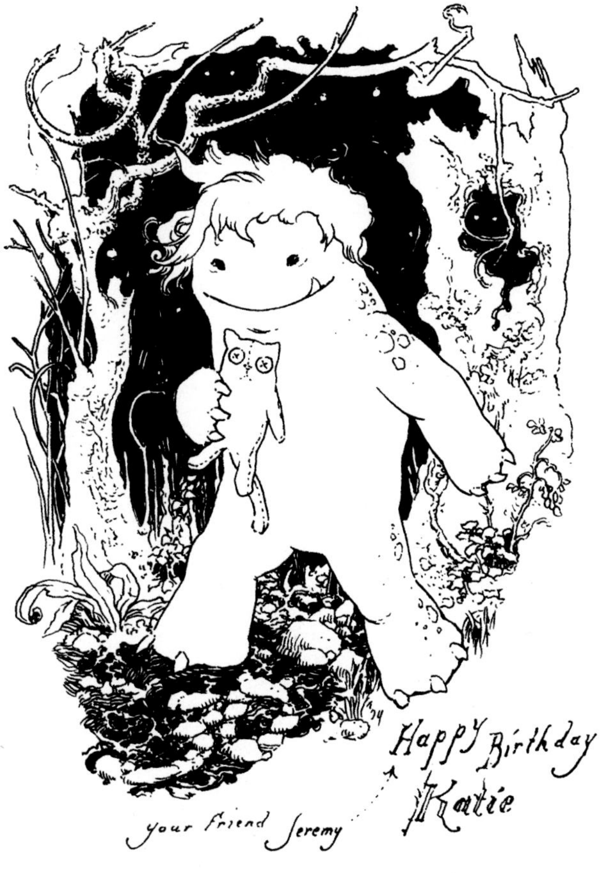
Happy Birthday Katie
your friend Jeremy

art by michael perez (aka meeks oddities)

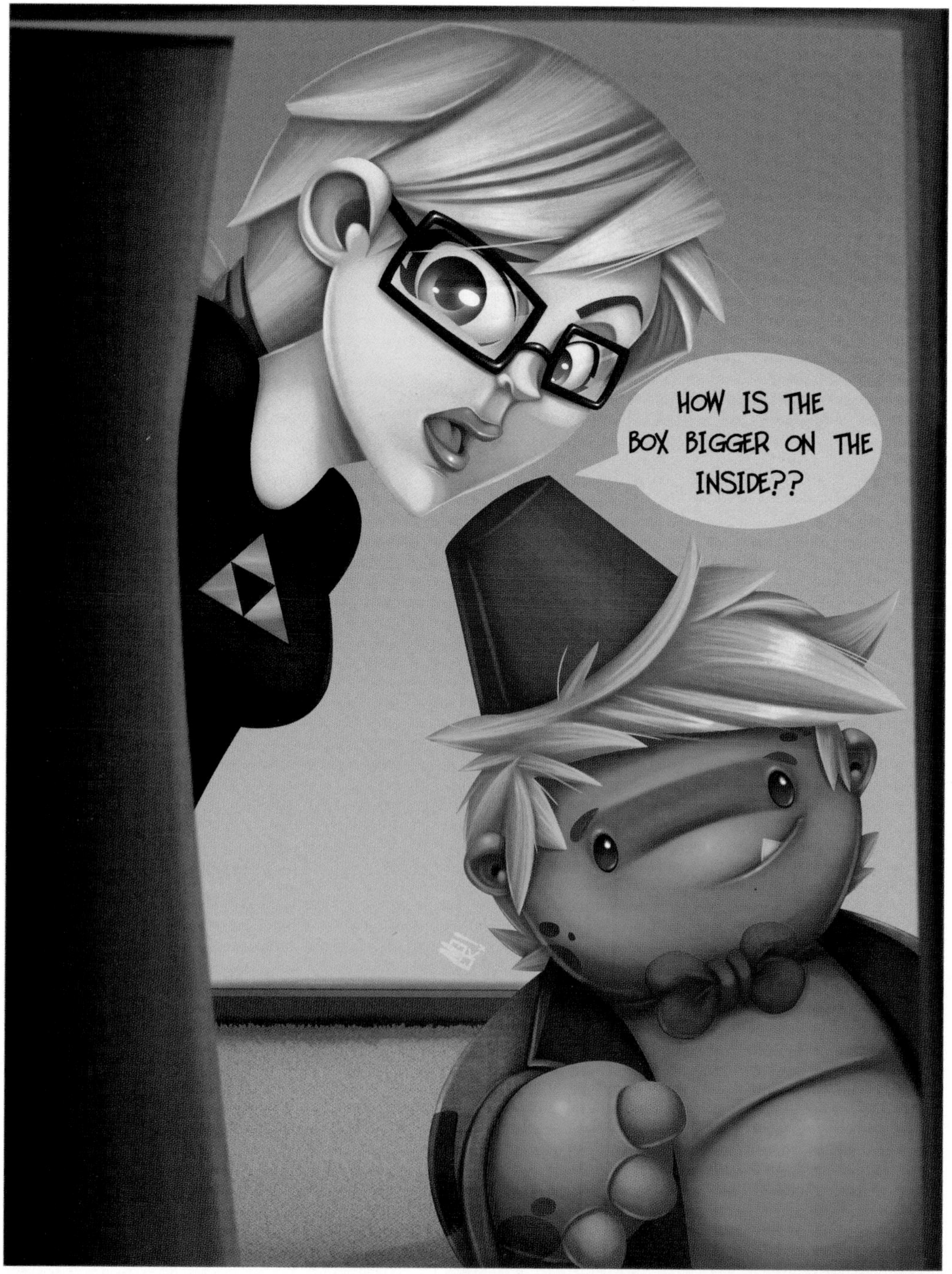
HOW IS THE BOX BIGGER ON THE INSIDE??

art by matt nelson

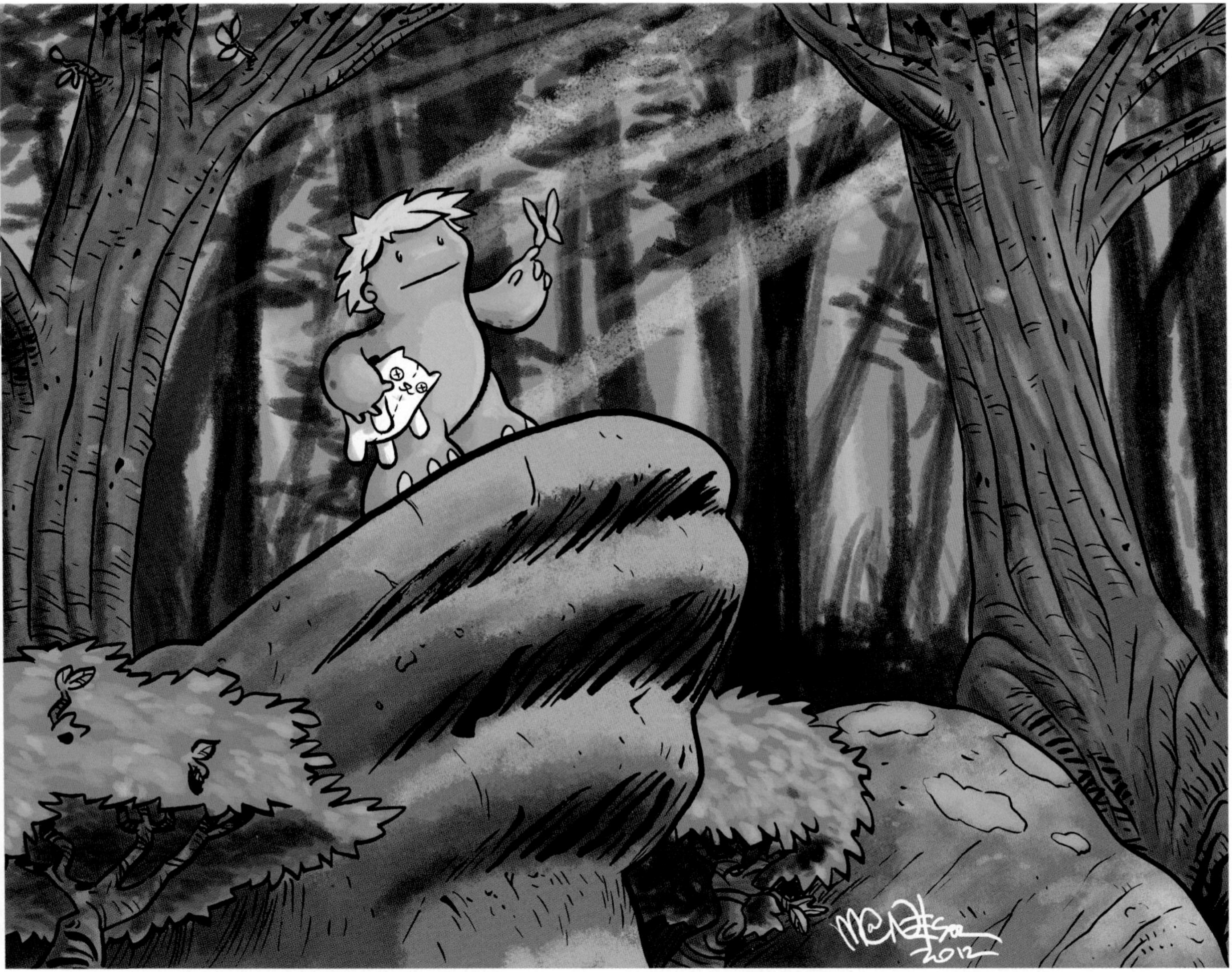

art by deanna piotrowski

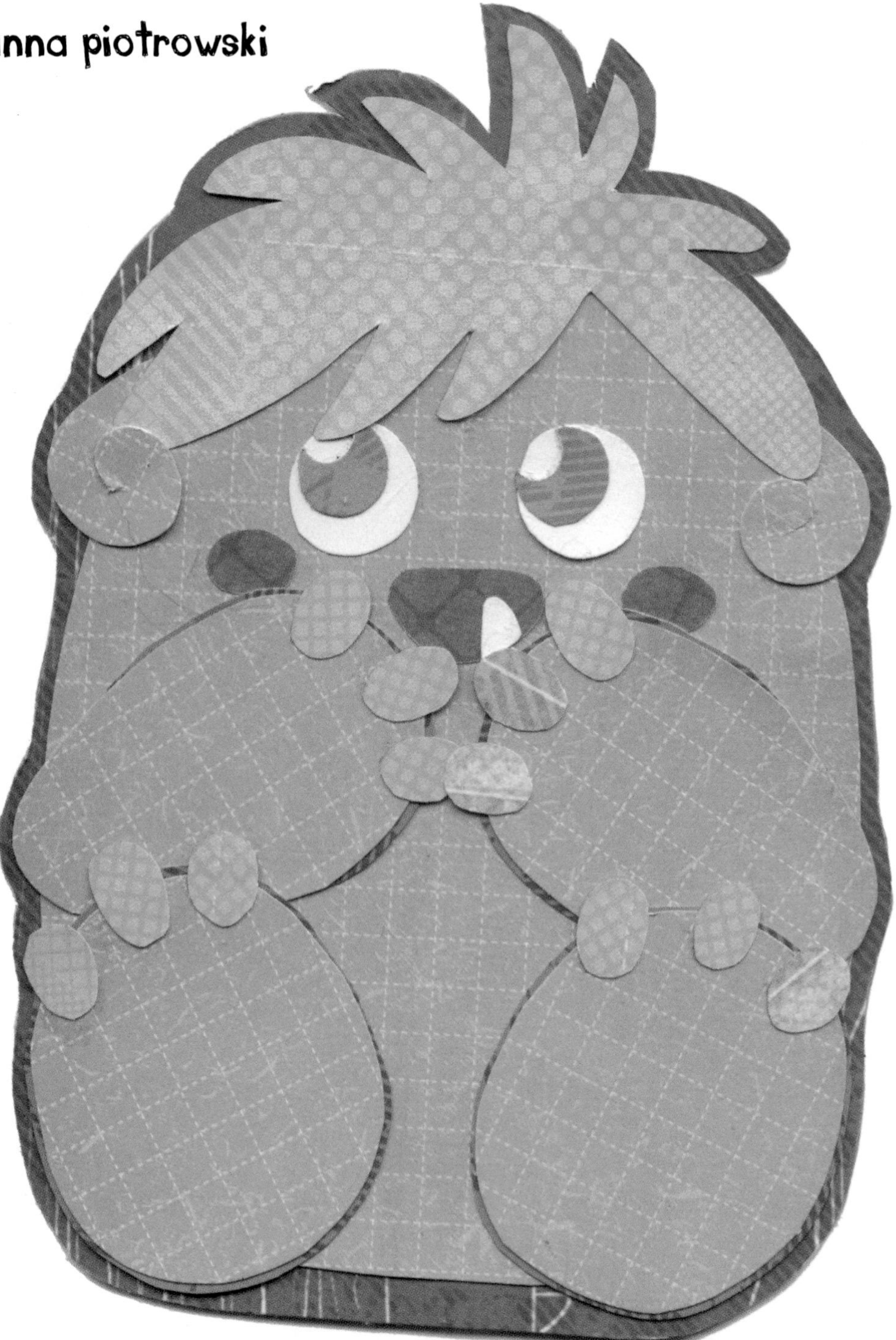

art by sean dove

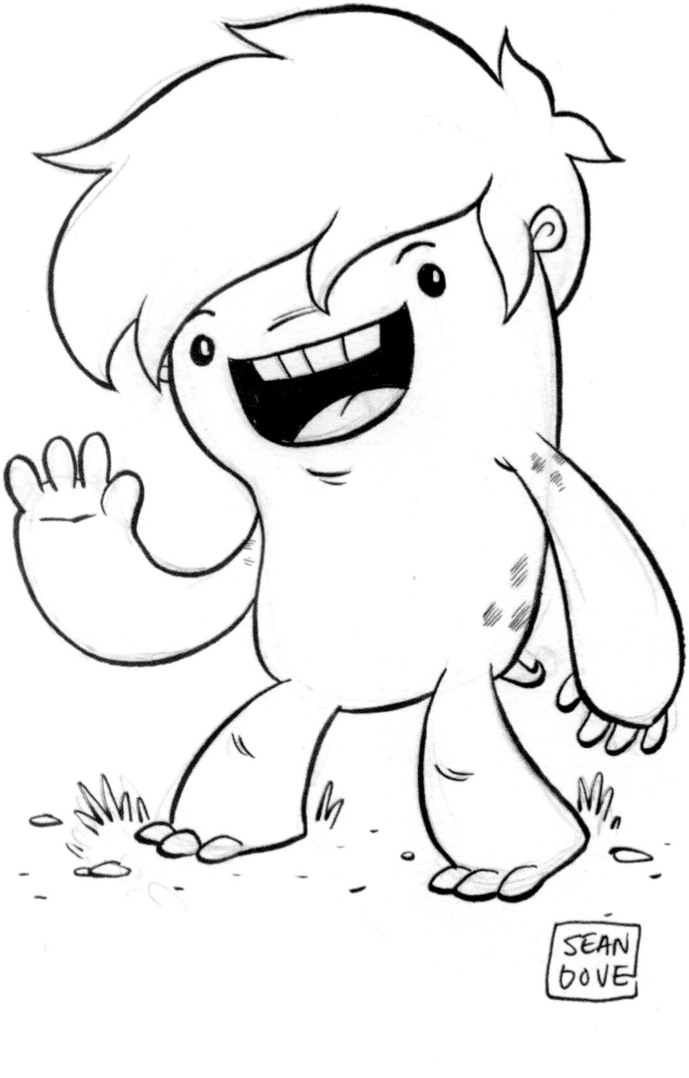
SEAN
DOVE

from my own sketchbook... gronk goes to london

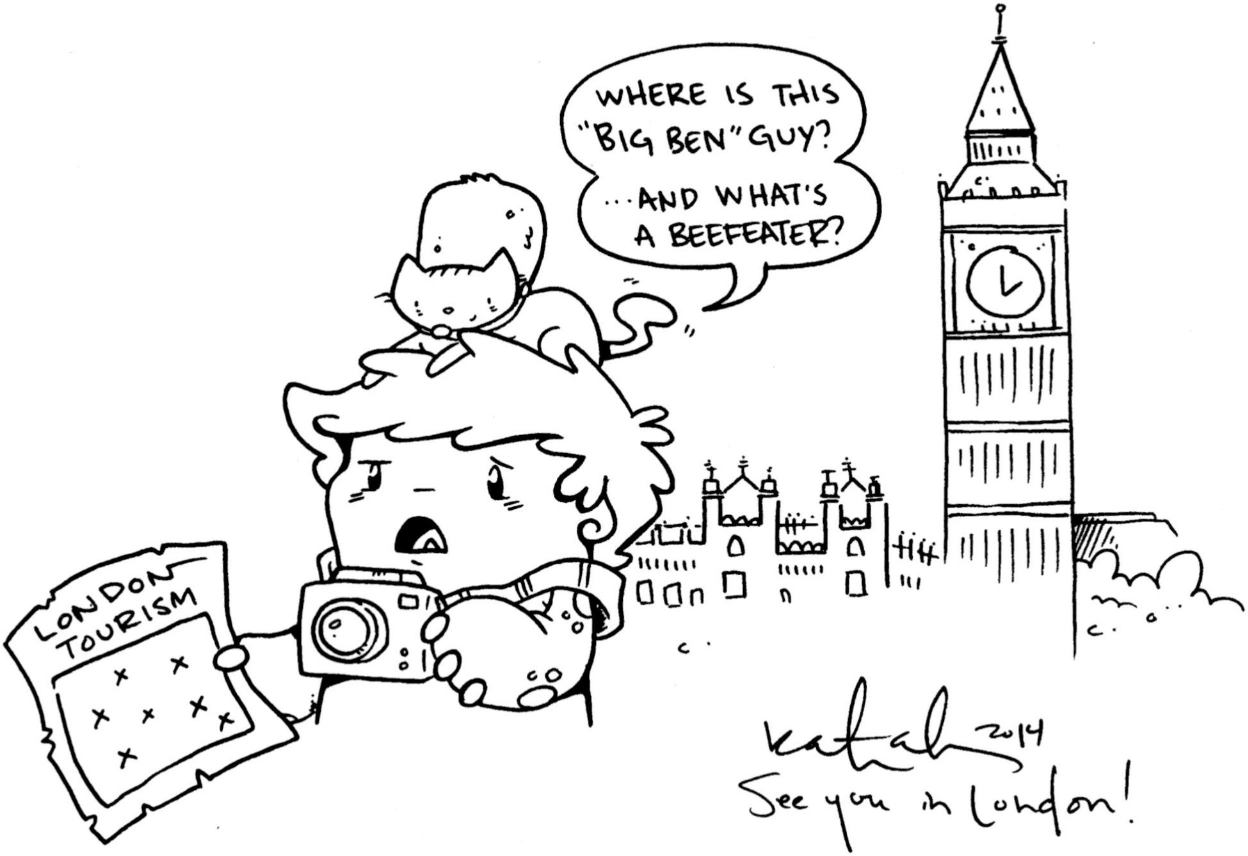

WHERE IS THIS "BIG BEN" GUY?
...AND WHAT'S A BEEFEATER?
LONDON TOURISM
katah 2014
See you in London!

from my own sketchbook...

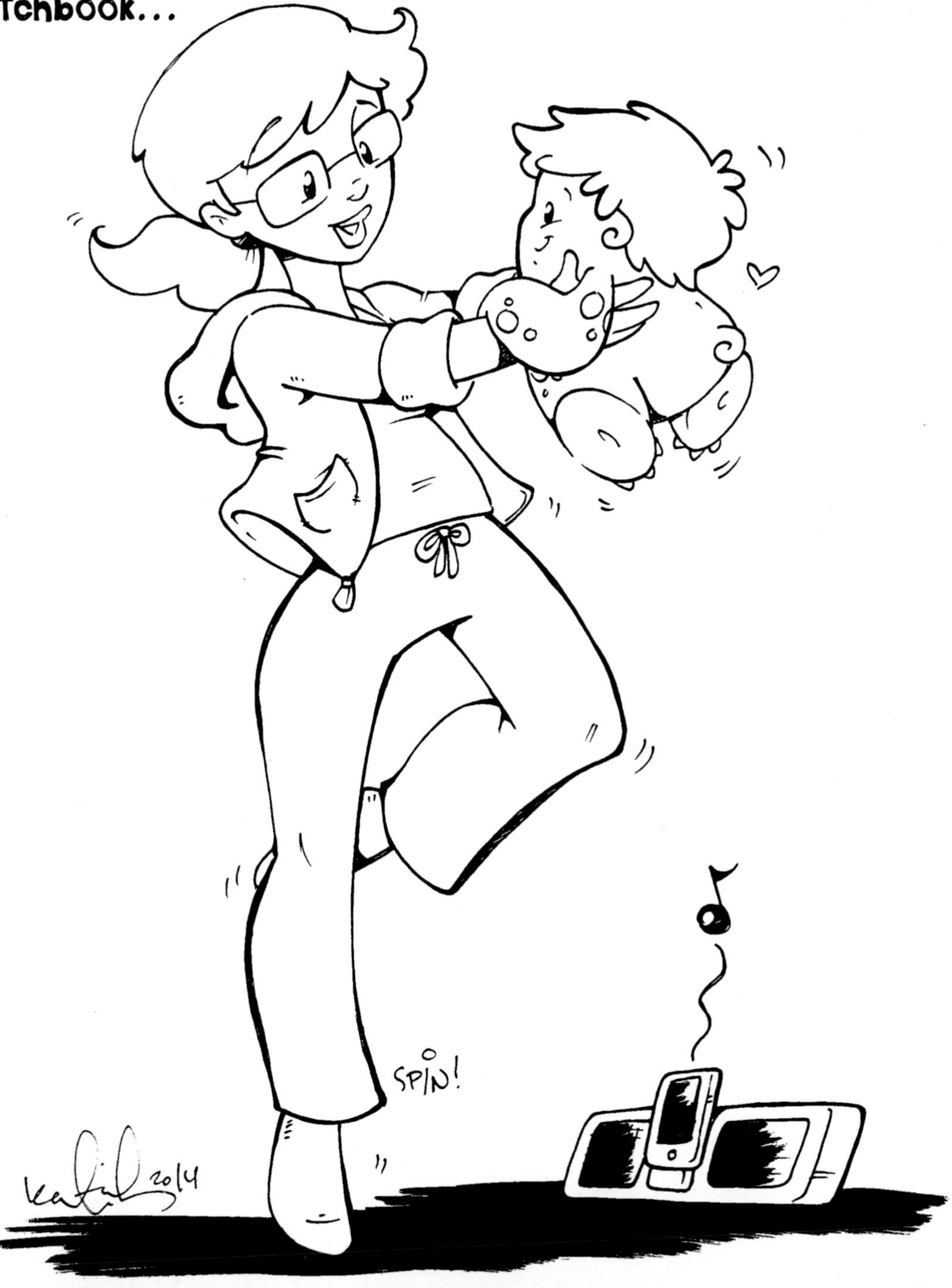
SPIN!
2014

from my own sketchbook...

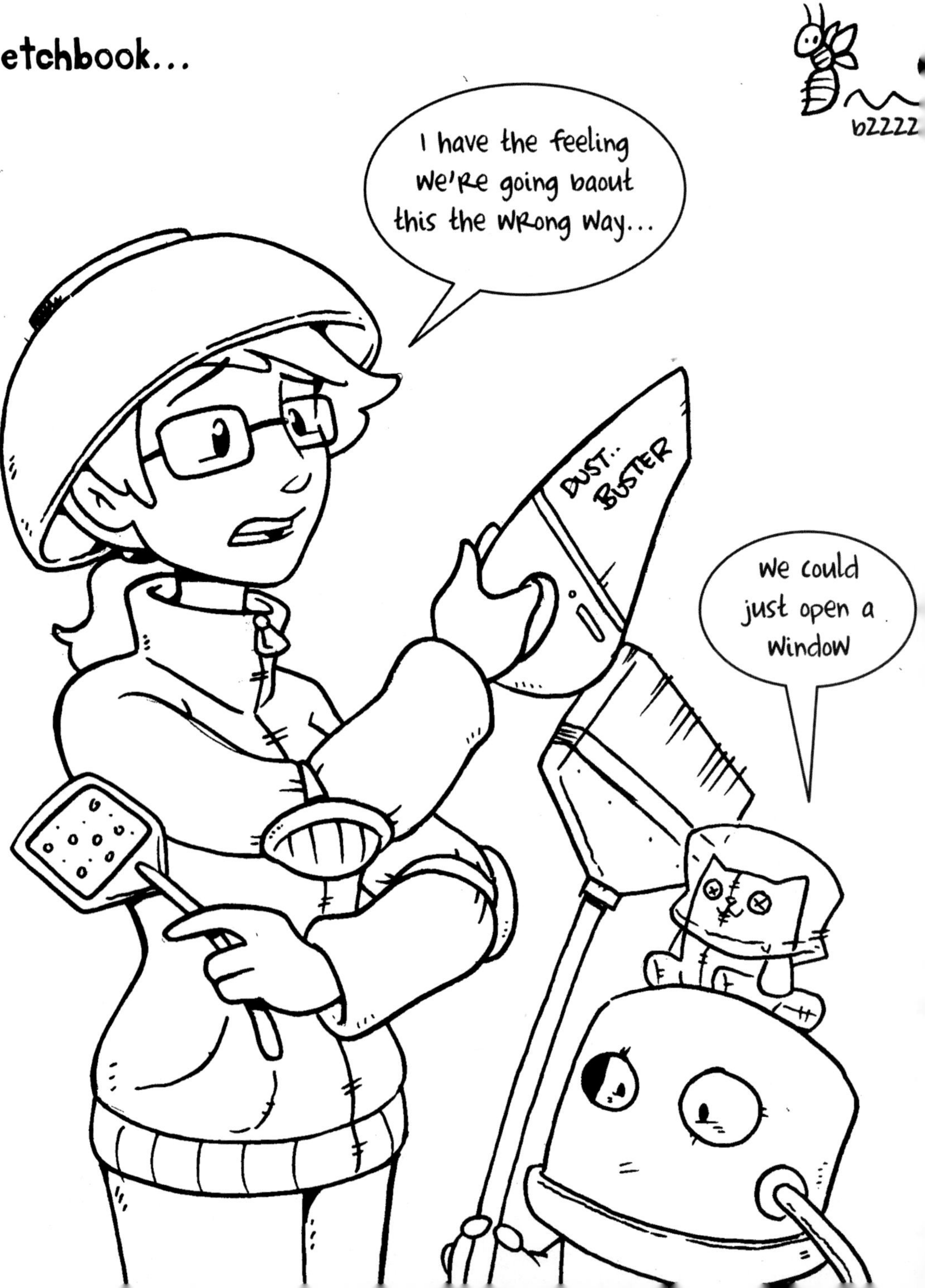
bzzzz
I have the feeling we're going baout this the wrong way...
DUST.. BUSTER
we could just open a window

from my own sketchbook...

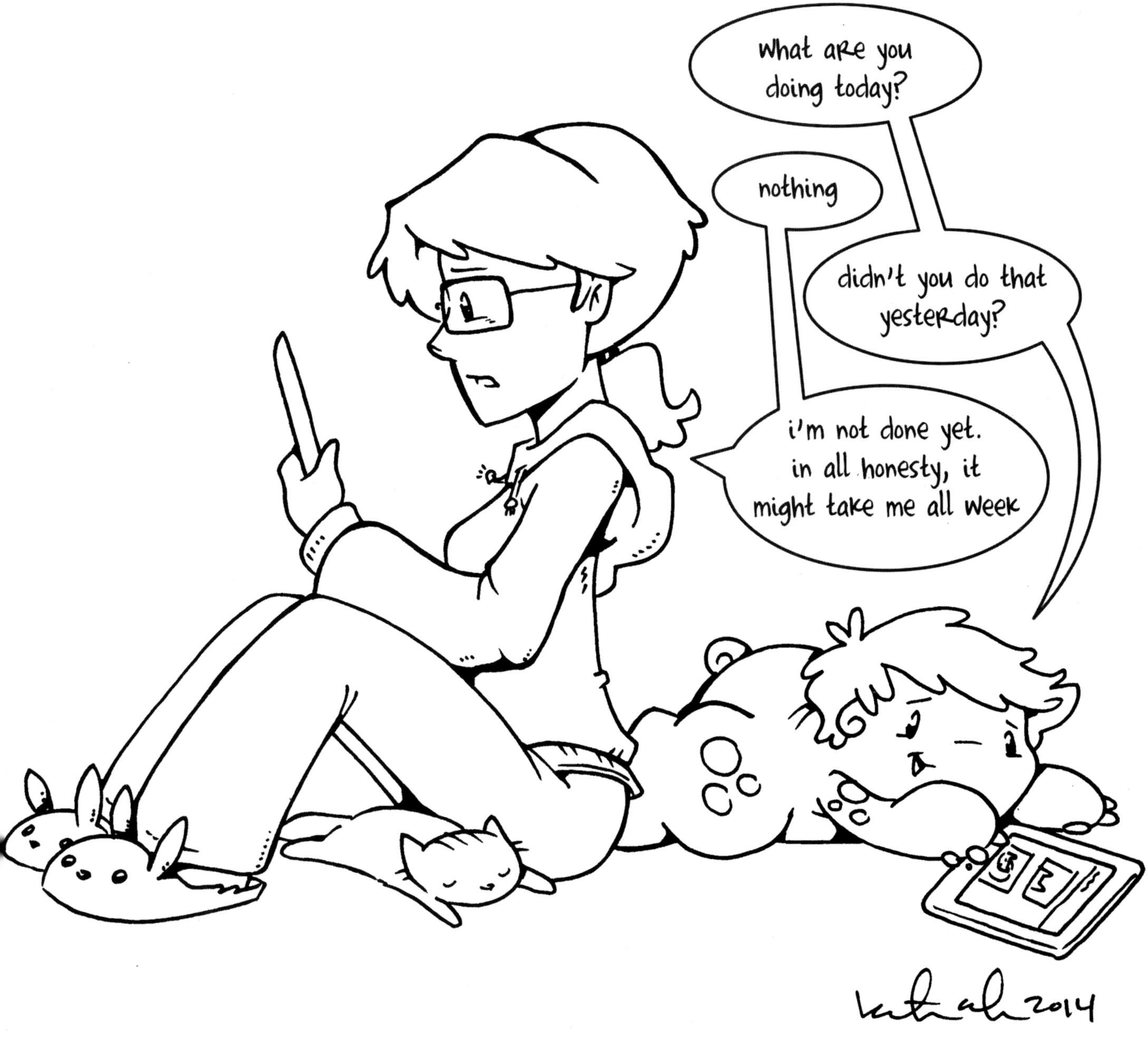
what are you doing today?
nothing
didn't you do that yesterday?
i'm not done yet. in all honesty, it might take me all week
katrah 2014

from my own sketchbook...

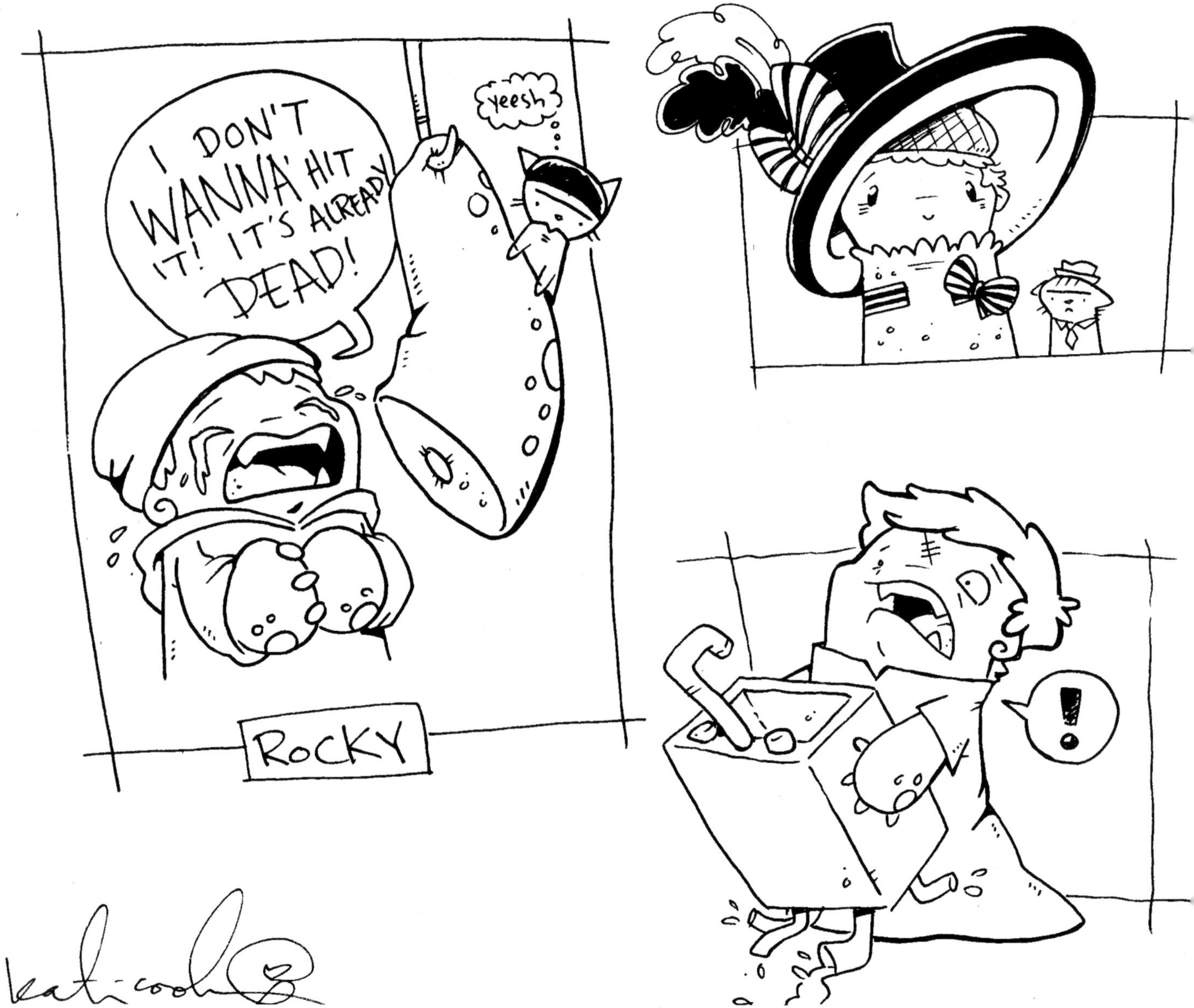
I DON'T WANNA' HIT IT! IT'S ALREADY DEAD!
yeesh
ROCKY
!

from my own sketchbook... what my comic thumbnails look like

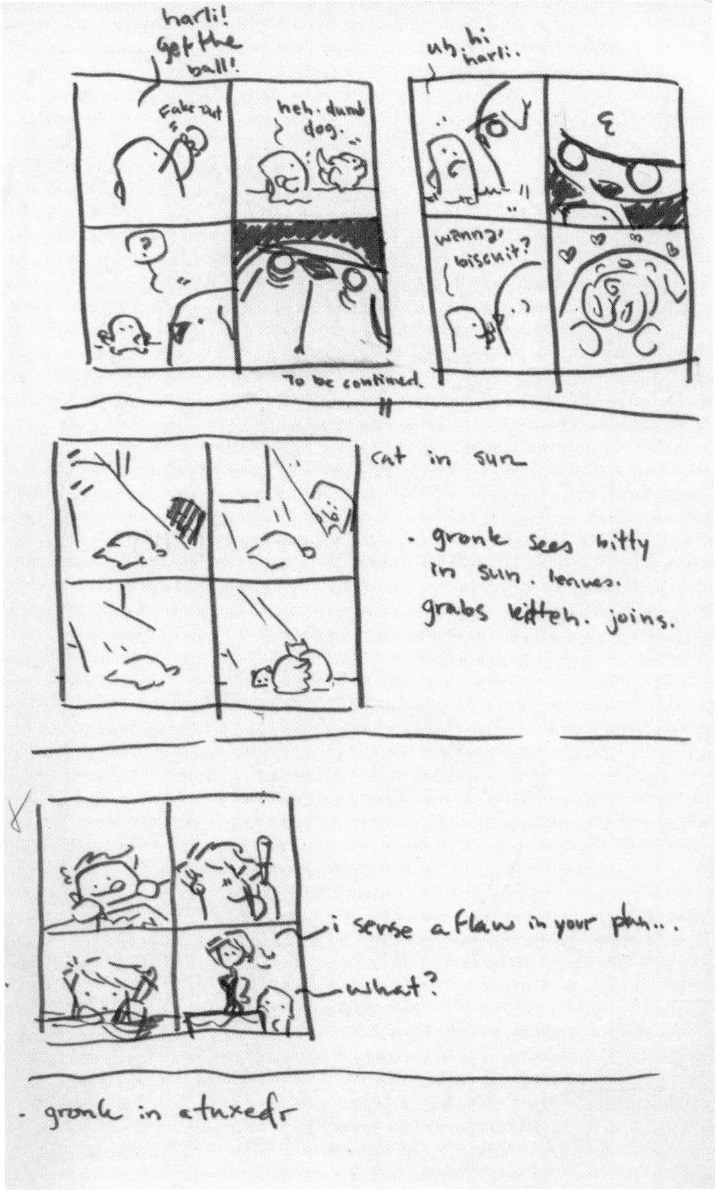
harli! get the ball!
fake out
heh. dumb dog.
uh, hi harli..
wanna biscuit?
To be continued.
cat in sun
· gronk sees kitty in sun. leaves. grabs kitteh. joins.
i sense a flaw in your plan...
what?
· gronk in a tuxedo

from my own sketchbook... really, this is how i plan a comic.

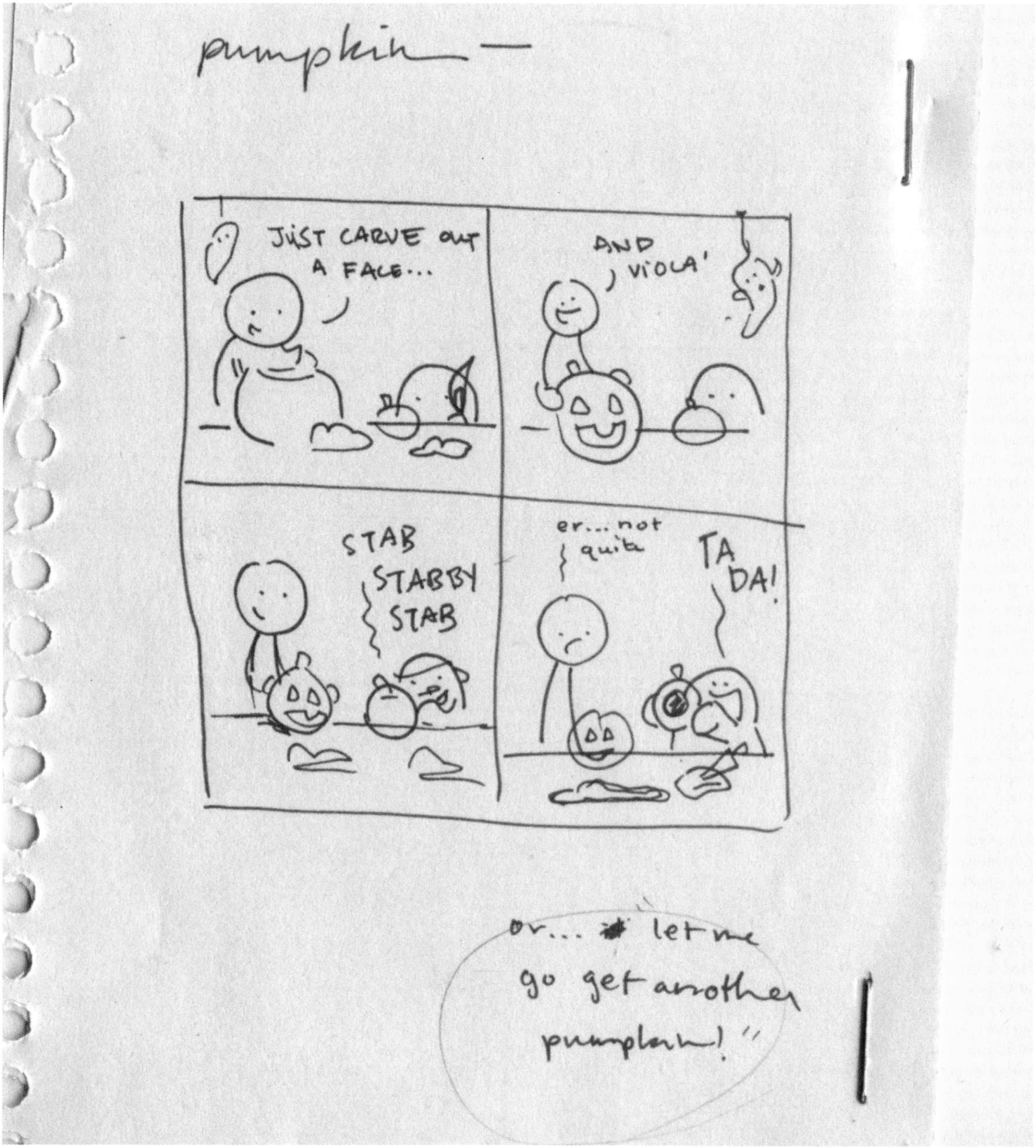

pumpkin —
JUST CARVE OUT A FACE...
AND VIOLA'
STAB STABBY STAB
er... not quite
TA DA!
or... let me go get another pumpkin!"

from my own sketchbook... notice the cat hair

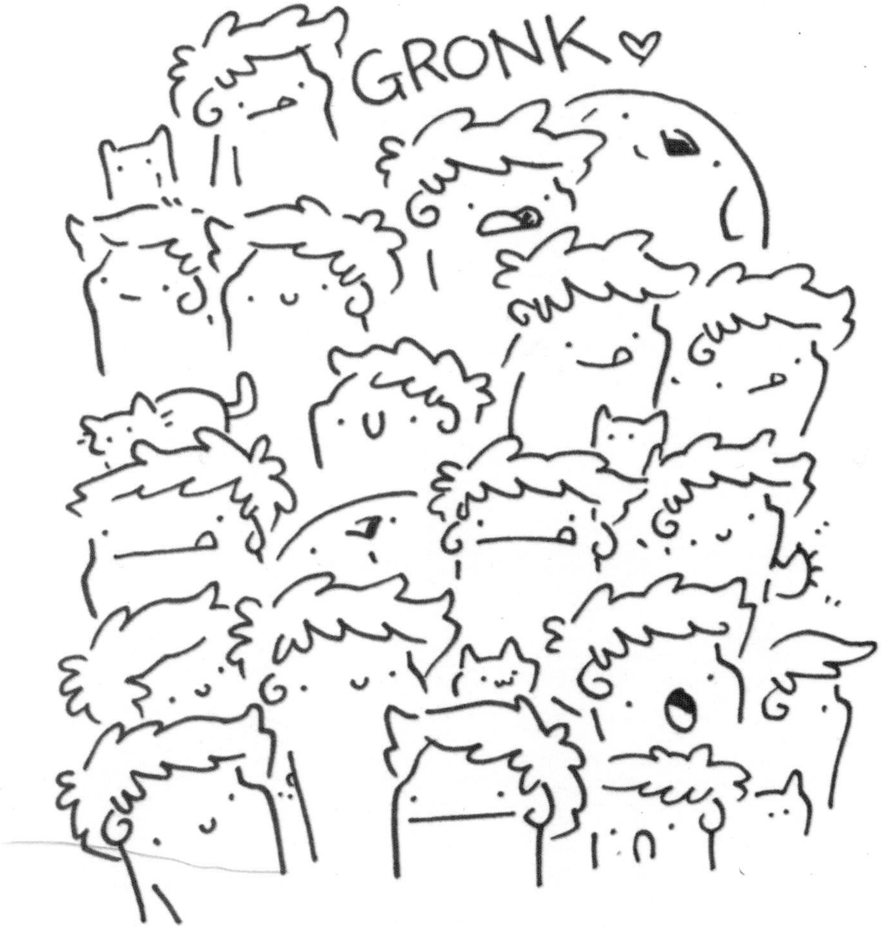
GRONK ♥

GRONK

a comic
katie co

a monster's story

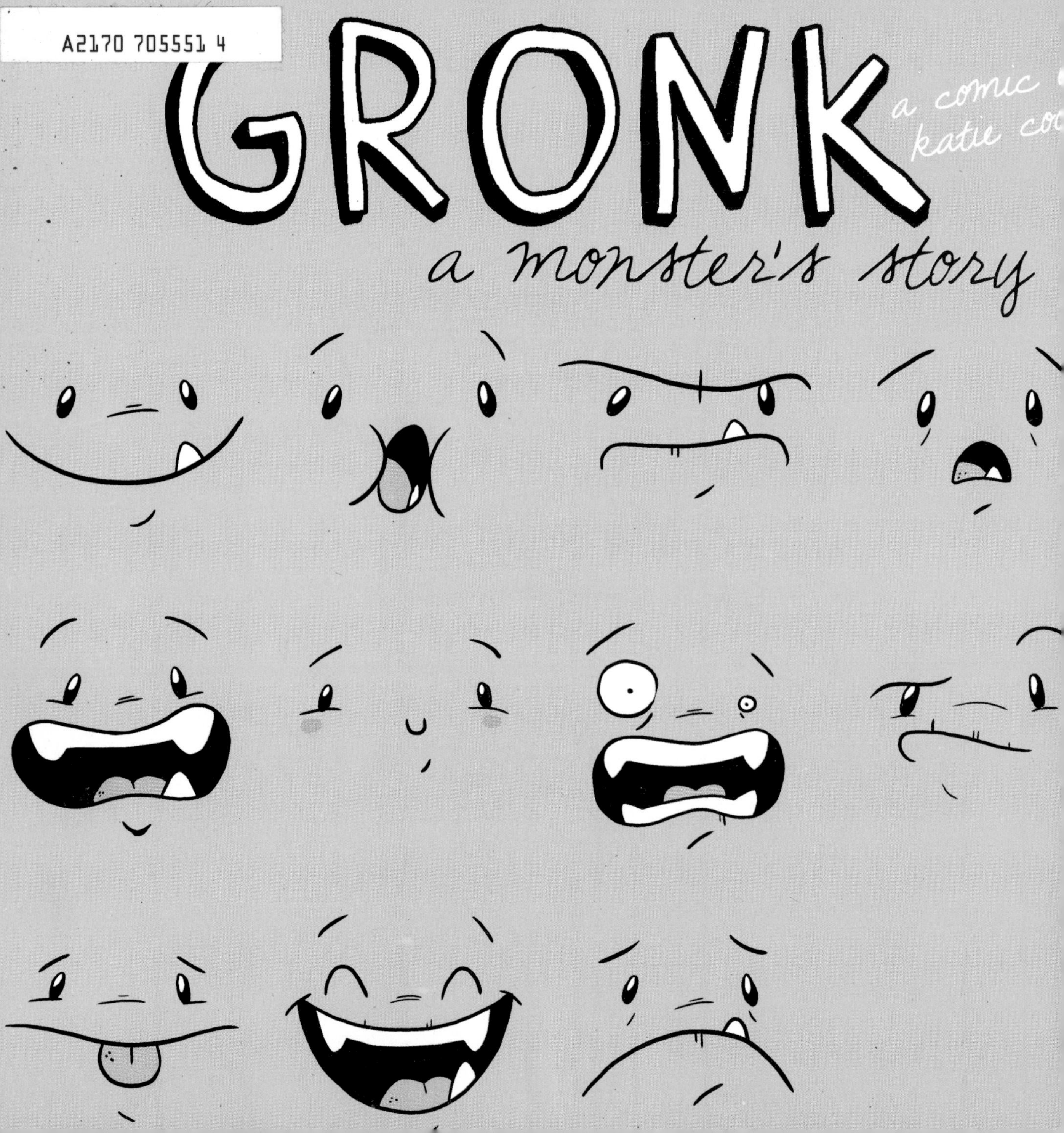